Simon Corrigan was born in Barnsley in 1964 and studied English at Cambridge and Hungarian Studies at the Sorbonne. He spent two years as a lecturer at the University of Budapest and currently lives in Portugal.

Also by Simon Corrigan

TOMMY WAS HERE

SWEETS FROM STRANGERS

SIMON CORRIGAN

It may not amount to a hill of
beans in this crazy world,
but will always have Brussels.

With much love

Simon xx

An *Abacus* Book

First published in Great Britain by André Deutsch Limited in 1994
This edition published by Abacus in 1995

Copyright © Simon Corrigan 1994

The moral right of the author has been asserted.

A CIP catalogue record for this book is available from the
British Library.

ISBN 0 349 10677 0

Printed and bound in Great Britain by Clays Ltd, St Ives plc

Abacus
A Division of
Little, Brown and Company (UK)
Brettenham House
Lancaster Place
London WC2E 7EN

For Julian Sperry,

with thanks and love

Contents

Some day, maybe, there will exist a well-informed, well-considered, and yet fervent conviction that the most deadly of all possible sins is the mutilation of a child's spirit; for such mutilation undercuts the life principle of trust, without which every human act, may it feel ever so good, and seem ever so right, is prone to perversion by destructive forms of consciousness.

Erik Erikson

Nor Am I Out
of It

Daniel was sitting in the brasserie called Galaxie in the Gare du Nord, on what they fondly call a terrace although it is indoors, and from where instead of watching the world go by you can watch it arrive and depart. At ten past eleven the hysterical woman appeared, weaving between the tables, much worse for wear and the past evening than he. Daniel transferred his travelling bag from the chair to the ground. The woman slipped into the empty seat beside him, removed the dark glasses, and began a hasty reconstruction of her make-up in her compact mirror.

Daniel watched this process without embarrassment; even with a certain scientific curiosity. 'Your hands are shaking,' he observed as she took up her eyeliner. 'You'll only make it worse.' She was digging away with the little pencil in her anxiety to make the line firm.

She spoke through her teeth. 'Don't patronise me.'

'I'm not patronising you. How am I patronising you?' She went on digging, digging with the little black pencil. 'Let me get you something to drink, at least.'

'Look.' She closed her fist around the pencil and turned to stare at him, but the eyeliner was making her blink. 'I don't need a drink,' she said. Even so she whispered a few seconds later: 'All right, then, you can get me a beer.'

Daniel looked out over the mournful platforms. Somewhere out there was his train. His mouth was dry; he too was suffering from the previous night. A farewell party they had called it: some farewell party, in a cellar bar with a

1

crowd of people he had known for a few hours, the unfamiliar faces staring into his own: 'So *you're* Daniel then? Well,
goodbye, goodbye.' Now, as the waiter approached, the
woman put on her dark glasses and Daniel said with jaunty
malice: 'What's the matter, are you scared of being recognised?' – though this was not unreasonable and she quite
famous in her way. She bent her head until the reddish hair
curtained her face and touched the table. She wore the fur
coat even now in balmy September, and it hung open about
her, symbolically, as if it were her own flayed hide.

He reached across and brushed away a few flakes of
cigarette ash from the tips of her hair. He began to laugh.
She lifted her head and demanded: 'What's so funny?'

His hand became tenderly still. 'It's your beret, it's falling
off.'

'Don't touch me.'

After a moment she commanded a cigarette and began to
talk, the familiar litany of complaints and recriminations,
not all of them directed against him. Her voice rose, raw,
over the tables: after taking such pains to preserve anonymity she now displayed a reckless indifference to attention.
Inevitably she began to cry, delved blindly into her bag. He
guided her twitching beringed fingers to a fresh packet of
Kleenex. She thanked him, tonelessly, and sat there dabbing
her eyes. 'I told you there was no point,' he said. 'I mean,
with the make-up.'

'You used to be so nice,' she said again, bending her
head, while he, watching her, considered in an altogether
detached manner his own impulse of a moment ago to bend
it still further, to take her by the back of the neck and hold
her face down amidst the debris of the table. Her fragility
was astounding. It would be like wringing the neck of a
chicken: disagreeable but altogether within the bounds of
capability. He shuddered and looked at his watch, then up
in disbelief to the many clocks around the station concourse,
the grey haze of the roof, the echoes: it was like being trap-
ped inside one's own hangover. His despairing boredom

2

was quite obvious; she saw it and made one last stab at conversation. 'So who knows you're going?'

'Just about everyone, I imagine.'

'Yes,' she confirmed. 'And who knows *where* you're going?'

'No one, I hope.'

She smiled. Lines previously unsuspected – or were they fresh? – crinkled into view. 'Very convenient. Leaving others to pick up the pieces. You really don't deserve to get off so lightly. Does Carlos know you're going?'

'I expect Luc will have told him. I said not to but I never really believed he wouldn't. You don't tell your secrets to Luc.' He squinted across at a crowd of people who were dispersing from around one of the ticket barriers. 'There's Luc now,' he said, surprised at the pleasure in his own voice, for he did not really want to speak to Luc and had no intention of signalling to him. 'Over there. I wonder what he's doing here.' And there Luc was: an absurdly good-looking boy leaning against a railing, absorbed in a newspaper. His head was bent, his hair flopped down over his eyes, nevertheless it was impossible not to recognise him: he lolled against the station railing as if he owned the place. As they watched him with the curiosity of pedestrians witnessing an accident or arrest, Luc took out a cigarette, lit it, and replaced the packet in his trousers all with one hand and without taking his eyes off the newspaper. 'I wonder what he's doing here,' Daniel repeated.

'He's been hanging around,' muttered the woman. Something in her speech caused him to glance over at her: she was sinking. It was not the effect of the beer so much as the fact of having not properly sobered up in the first place. Why ever did I get involved with this woman? he asked himself. She was never more than peripheral. And yet, and yet, though she called herself old, a wreck, a shell, still there was something quite splendid about her, some flicker of the woman she had been. He felt a warm great tenderness for her, but it was a regretful tenderness, like the recollection of someone who has died. He pulled himself together and

3

concentrated on the waiting trains, one of which was his. He was going home, but he was also running away.

She spoke suddenly out of whatever depths she wandered. 'He's talking to that man. Look. What d'you think he's up to now?'

'I don't think he knows we're here.'

'He'd know all right. What will you do when you get there?'

He sat back and folded his arms across his chest. 'First,' he said, 'I'll buy all the Sunday newspapers and take them into a pub and drink as many pints of beer as I can afford. Then,' dropping his voice so she was obliged to listen in closer, 'then I'll pick up the first halfway decent girl who comes along. Then I'll take a long bath and spend three years watching television and drinking tea, one year for every year out here in hell. And then, then, I might just write you a letter.' He was whispering now, it might almost have been hushed endearments that he breathed into her hair.

She roused herself, reached into her bag and brought out a small, beautifully wrapped package. 'It's for you.'

He took it in his hands, unsure quite what to do with it. 'Should I open it now?' He removed the expensive shiny wrapping. Inside the black box was a gold watch made by Raymond Weil of Geneva. He asked: 'Is this the pay-off?'

She turned her face away. 'There's no need to be quite so cruel. After all, you're the one who's leaving.'

'I'm sorry,' he said. 'It's beautiful. Thank you.' He took it out of the box and weighed it over his forefinger. He looked up to see Luc moving off with the other man, then his view was obscured by a station employee shouting as he drove his luggage wagons into the heart of the crowd. Looking down at the grains of coffee in his cup he wished he had had something stronger; several of something stronger. The only way to travel is drunk, he reminded himself. There's no danger in being drunk if you're moving.

Eyes closed, she said: 'So where's this famous train of yours?'

He had no intention of letting her stay. 'It's out there. There's another fifteen minutes. I think I'd better get you into a taxi.' She was wilting again; in a few moments she would be asleep there on the café table. He asked two youngish men at a nearby table to watch over his bag, then lifted her from her seat and steered her towards an exit. He felt the heavy furs dragging at her, a deadweight slung over her shoulders. Outside the station was a line of taxis. To the first driver he gave the address and with exaggerated gravity explained: 'The lady is ill, she has a touch of sunstroke, please take care of her.' His haste to be done with her was almost indecent.

Back in the station he found a payphone that worked and called England. 'Just to say I'm leaving in ten minutes. I get into London about seven this evening, your time. I'll call you from there.' Cradling the receiver on his shoulder he removed his old wristwatch, itself a fairly recent gift, and slipped on the new one.

They were announcing the departure of his train. He went back for his bag, thanked the two men and turned away, then, on an impulse, returned to the table. 'Do either of you want a watch?' he said. 'I don't need it any more. It's quite new, I only had it a year, maybe just over a year. Look, it's quite a good one . . .'

He dangled it in front of their faces, all the while explaining what a fine watch it was. They didn't understand, thought he must be trying to sell it to them, they interpreted his enthusiasm as straight hustling, but the more sceptical they appeared and the more hostile, the more fulsomely he sought to extol the virtues of his watch. Finally one of them said with unmistakable menace: 'Look, kid, nobody wants your watch. I've got a watch, we've both got watches. Thanks and all that, just drop it, okay?'

A train was shrieking imperatively and Daniel turned his head. He walked over to a litter bin twelve feet away and dropped the old watch inside. One of the men stood up from the table and called after him: 'Hey, just a minute . . .' But he was running now, pushing his way through a throng

5

of Italian schoolchildren who crowded round the gateway. With delight he observed the woman's gift glinting on his wrist as it caught the dirty Paris light that filtered through the old glass of the roof. A new watch for an old time zone. How symbolic, he thought with pleasurable irony, remembering that it was from her he had picked up this habit of finding symbols everywhere: in watches, in stations, in ash on a woman's hair. He hauled himself up onto the train. He was running away, but he was also going home.

Or something approaching. Three weeks before, out of the blue, he had telephoned his sister Rachel. 'I'm coming back to England. I mean, for good. I want to get a job and lead a normal life. I want a new start. I can't go and live with the parents. Can I stay with you? Just for a few weeks, just till I'm settled and find something.'

'Do they know? Have you told them about this?'

'Not yet. Don't say anything. Please.'

They had none of them seen him for over two years, during which time Rachel had watched her own position in the family change from that of the problematic, ingrate, rebel first-born to one of a near-respectable, if frequently misguided, daughter. This partial rehabilitation had operated in direct proportion to the worsening of relations between her parents and Daniel, the former blue-eyed boy, since in that family – even in that family – there was room for only one out-and-out villain at a time.

It must be said all the same that what Daniel had done was beyond the pale: two years out of three completed at Cambridge, a summer jaunt in France, and then the glittering prizes jettisoned every one, and with them, it seemed, his family. He didn't want a degree, he wasn't going back to university, he was finished with England and set on a new life in Europe. All this he announced in a frantic, scarcely coherent letter to his parents, on numerous sheets of the headed notepaper of a Paris hotel whose address, now, was the only reference they had for him.

He didn't sever all connection with his family, not then: that was to come the following year, when he granted them not even the address of some tawdry hotel. No: in those first months he was quite regular with calls to his parents or his sister, on occasion going so far as to pen a few lines on a postcard, reporting on his progress, his new job, his apartment. They resigned themselves to his absence, wrote it off as the caprice of a retarded adolescence. It was assumed he would come to his senses in time.

The next summer Daniel returned to England for a projected three-week visit, a disaster from the start. His physical and mental state utterly belied those hubristic dispatches from Paris: he was hysterically touchy, antagonistic, loudly inarticulate with fury. There were interminable rows; afterwards he would skulk off to a pub for hours, or rudely, defiantly, telephone his friends abroad and continue a conversation, in French, for his parents to overhear. At the end of the first week he fled to the house of his sister and her husband in Norwich, but fared little better there. Rachel was heavily pregnant with her third child and disinclined to take sides in a new family conflict, nor was she equal to coping with whatever black demons Daniel had imported. Furthermore it transpired that he had not even the money to pay his return fare to Paris, and was obliged to beg it of the parents he had just abandoned, for Rachel had none to give him.

In a mood of definite crisis Mr and Mrs Marriner descended on Rachel's house, and there was a sticky reconciliation of sorts around the dinner table through most of which Daniel sat with bowed head and shoulders set in an attitude of suitable penitence, for he really did need his fare back to Paris and anything else on offer besides. Rachel found her role of mediator rather thankless, gave up trying, and contented herself with making rounds of coffee and sandwiches for the unwanted guests. Guy, seven years old, her eldest child by an earlier disgraceful liaison, kept out of

7

the way as much as possible, although he was heard to enquire, after one particularly strident scene, with reference to Daniel: 'Mummy, when is he going away?'

On his last night, when their parents were slumbering overhead, Daniel sat in the kitchen while Rachel cleared away. He watched her glumly as she moved about, slow in her eighth month, stacking plates, collecting and sorting the children's laundry. He said: 'Rachel, I've screwed up. I'm sorry.'

She didn't want to be drawn into any discussion; was impatient, as the new child stretched for life within her, to be alone again and free of her morbid family with its fears and past-rooted preoccupations. Yes, she felt sorry for Daniel, but like the money she would gladly have offered but hadn't to spare, such concern would have depleted her own precious reserves now when all her energies were needed. She said: 'Don't think about it, don't give it another thought.' Next morning they all drove to the station for Daniel's train to London. Baby Karl was the only one with a smile, and that was for the fascinating trains and the railway employees in their gleaming uniforms. Daniel said his goodbyes, set off back for the Continent and for two years never set foot in England, at least that anyone knew.

In the bar of a hotel not far from Victoria Station Daniel was drinking amidst a smattering of hotel guests, in-transit continental travellers and assorted individuals who, for whatever reason, were out in this charmless half-life district of London on a Sunday evening in summer. With its bland shabby luxury, unnecessary expensiveness, its waiting-room anonymity, and with the murmur of foreign languages and accents around him, the bar seemed a fitting place in which to toast his return to England.

'Here is my house in Paris,' he told the Italian couple, the honeymooners, part of a whole honeymoon grand package tour of Europe. Then, with exaggerated labour, he repeated in Italian: '*Ecco la mia casa, a Parigi.*' He was passing around the half dozen or so photographs he kept, from habit alone, in his wallet.

The couple nodded their appreciation and examined the picture. They were too stunned by the rigours of the journey, too absorbed in the novelty of each other, finally too untutored in the English language to notice anything odd in Daniel's behaviour, in his shining eyes, his gleaming cheeks, in his strong-arm adoption of them during the crossing and again as they stood, indecisive amidst the luggage, at Victoria Station. 'No, no,' they had murmured soothingly as Daniel pressed them to accept drinks, 'oh no, thank you – '; but their reluctance was half-hearted, indifferent.

He made them examine each one of the photos. 'This is my street . . . this is me on the steps of Trocadéro, with my friends from the Sorbonne . . . this is my fiancée . . .' At the word fiancée, bride and groom turned from their host as one and beamed into each other's faces: too naïve, too uncomprehending to reject him as a bore or account him a menace. 'My fiancée,' he was saying loudly, 'my fiancée bought me this watch, on my twenty-first birthday, in the Place Vendôme in Paris. It's a Raymond Weil watch, from Geneva in Switzerland; they are not as showy as Rolex nor so "snob" as Cartier. It is a perfect reflection of her taste and my own.'

The Italian girl appeared suddenly to recall that they were engaged in conversation, and dutifully ventured: 'We were in the Place Vendôme also when the tour went to Paris, but we were sight-seeing only, of course.'

And the husband supplied: 'You must be happy to be again in England, after all this time. You have not missed your family?'

Daniel's eyes closed momentarily. 'My parents are dead.' He opened them again. 'You have a room in this hotel?'

The husband was waving to another Italian, also of the tour party, who had signalled to them from the bar. To Daniel's repeated question he replied distractedly: 'Yes. Oh yes.'

The wife now waved over to their colleagues at the bar. She turned back to Daniel, evidently ill at ease with the intrusive intimacy of his smile. 'Our friends, you see.'

Daniel looked from the one to the other with a generalised sadness, near to sympathy. 'Am I boring you?' he said.

They made their conventional protests, sought to reassure him. But Daniel was on his feet already, as if wounded beyond endurance, gathering up his bag, stuffing the bundle of his coat under one arm: his eyes were bright, his face flushed, as he convinced himself, more and more, of the deep offence he had just suffered at the hands of these strangers. He hurried from the bar, from the hotel, and out into the buoyant evening air of Grosvenor Gardens, pausing on the pavement to consider his next move, aware of the incessant trembling of his hands. He had not slept for forty-eight hours.

Rachel lived with her husband and her three children in a rather ugly house in a pretty Oxfordshire town that straddled the Thames. It was not easy to say what constituted this ugliness, since the house had been built in the same late eighteenth century as its graceful neighbours, in a street often praised for its charm: something to do, perhaps, with the smallness of the windows and their distance one from another, like the features of a face too vacantly big for them.

Inside, the house exuded a different type of vacancy. None of the furnishings had been bought with these rooms in mind, but dated from the smaller lodgings of more cramped and less prosperous days; or else they were the inevitably mismatched discards of parents and relatives. The resultant aura of impermanence didn't bother Rachel, who was not house-proud in any usual sense of the word. Besides, the family had been uprooted too many times already; they would have been tempting fate to behave as if settled. In the five years since her marriage to Robert they had moved from Leeds to Sunderland, to another flat in Sunderland, to Norfolk, to London, and finally here.

Robert worked primarily in Oxford, sometimes in London, and was occasionally required to travel to Belgium. His career had been chequered and it was only in the last two years that they had had any money whatsoever. Once again, Rachel was relatively uninterested in the family finances, provided her children were clothed and fed, and debt where possible avoided. She often felt she would willingly have returned to the precarious existence of old if only Robert could have spent more time at home. She was not materialistic and in five years had acquired little in the way of possessions beyond the two dogs and two cats who, with the children, completed the household.

Guy was not Robert's child. He was in part at least the consequence of two separate but equally incorrect diagnoses by the same doctor. Rachel had been eighteen at the time, recovering from a quite trivial operation. The sentence passed on her, that she was unlikely ever to have children, had a disastrous effect, impelling her into a helter-skelter of hopeless, self-destructive affairs. The last of these, with a married lecturer acquaintance of her father, proved to be a screaming stand-up drama in the Marriner household, as well as a minor scandal in their circle, all the more so when Rachel discovered herself, incredibly, to be pregnant. The doctor then informed them, with only the merest trace of embarrassment over his earlier mistake, that this was almost certainly the only child Rachel would ever be able to bear. While there was no question of an abortion, no more was there of involving the craven father, now chastened into reconciliation with his wife, and anxious about his position in a neighbouring teacher-training college, where, to make matters worse, Rachel herself was a student. The news chastened Rachel, too, in a different way: she quite fell out of love with the man and determined to cut him out of her life and, in so far as was possible, out of the future life of her unborn child.

They were difficult years that followed. Rachel, while still nominally a student at the college, was obliged to live at home with her parents and commute to classes, since accommodation for students with children was severely limited. Inevitably her attendance was erratic, her work suffered: in the event she managed a degree unworthy of her, though even that achievement was little short of heroic. Her parents, still smarting from the ignominy, adapted badly to the presence of the baby. Its noise, its mess bothered Mr Marriner, plunging him into frequent taciturn moods punctuated by outbursts of rage; while Mrs Marriner, whose memory was short, found Guy an unnaturally troublesome and demanding child. Meantime Daniel passed sixteen and was wrangling with his own adolescent travails, all the more bitter in that he felt cheated of rightful attention by his sister and the baby.

Rachel found a part-time job as a receptionist in a nearby hotel. The work was dull and not well paid, but it got her out of the house and enabled her for a time to shoal up her shattered self-esteem, and with rigorous saving to rent a flat of her own. This she announced to a barrage of tears and recriminations, though the tiny flat was only twenty minutes' walk from her parents' house, since Rachel was still dependent on her mother's goodwill to juggle the demands of child and work. 'But if that's the case, why do you have to move out at all?' demanded Mrs Marriner, as if counting for nothing the constant disagreements with Rachel over the basics of the correct bringing up of Guy, or the baleful atmosphere produced by the shouting matches with Daniel, or the frequent, quite vicious spats between the parents themselves, indulged in regardless of whether Guy was in the room or not. Rachel had a very specific fantasy, one she could hardly impart to her mother: she wanted to finish her day's work, collect Guy from her parents', take him home, feed him, bathe him, put him to bed, and then enjoy a glass of red supermarket wine. It was this need more than anything that impelled her to leave home and rent a flat which, inexpensive as it was, represented a certain extravagance: the need to attend to her child and drink a glass of wine beyond the reach of criticism and dire prognosis.

Somehow, drawing on unsuspected reserves of strength and optimism, and because most things are survivable, she lived through it. Sometimes she worried about the future, and sometimes she dreamed of it – another job in another town, other qualifications, a career – but always she remembered her son, and how that eternally hypothetical future was a betrayal of her son and his actual needs, had nothing to do with him. Or rather, her son *was* the future, growing heedless of anxiety or yearning, solidly obdurate to both. Secretly, even guiltily, as if engaged in a conspiracy with herself, in the exhausted late evenings with her solitary glass of cheap wine, sitting in her ill-lit flat at a table piled high with laundry, she meditated on the reality of Guy and her own lack of freedom, and on her ultimate responsibility to shelter him as much from her own fears and doubts as from the demoralising strictures of her mother.

When she least expected it – for she never went out, had no occasion to meet people beyond her work – she met Robert. He was twelve years older than her, divorced, with a history of more or less successful ventures in the leisure and catering industry, the latest of which had brought him in itinerant capacity to the hotel where Rachel worked. For all the precariousness of his own existence he approached Rachel with, and offered her, an extreme calm, altogether unfazed as he was by her baby and her troubled antecedents. Unbeknown to the Marriners he moved into the flat, set about securing a quasi-permanent posting in the region, and three months later they were quietly married.

Shortly afterwards he lost his job, but to the cloud of redundancy there was for Rachel a silver lining: they would have to move to another part of the country, far away from her family. This move marked the beginning of their first period of dire poverty, when dinner was frequently no more than a can of soup, when they neglected to reconnect the telephone for fear of a call from their irate landlord, when Guy was the only one among them to have decent shoes or a new coat for the winter. But the gloom of these living conditions was altogether offset by the wonderful news: Rachel was pregnant again. By the time Karl was born, healthy, sturdy, resiliently jovial, unmistakably his father's child, they had moved to a nicer flat in Sunderland and were awaiting a still better posting to Norwich.

Daniel came to visit, bringing with him the rarefied air of his first year in Cambridge, about which he was still enthusiastic, suspiciously so. He and Rachel spoke a little about their parents and about the troubled last years at home: he went so far as to express regret for his own lack of understanding, his misplaced jealousy during Rachel's first pregnancy and motherhood. But he was clearly uninterested in Guy or the new baby, or in the dream of domesticity his sister sought to realise. He talked about his forthcoming trip to France as if it were the only thing worth doing or talking about. And though they parted on friendly terms, the letters through which they maintained contact were made up of news from two separate worlds, so alien and without significance the one to the other, that they might have been communicating in different languages.

It was a year later and Daniel had already fled to Paris, for good this time, he said, when Rachel announced she was pregnant with a third child. Their parents were not overjoyed; indeed, almost the first comment from Mrs Marriner was: 'Well, will there be room for *us* when we come down to stay?' She subsequently backtracked, and explained away her reluctance as anxiety over the young couple's financial state: could they *afford*, did they have *money* enough, for another baby? Three children struck her as extravagant, excessive, like a second car or an additional holiday.

And indeed, once again Robert found himself out of a job and they were obliged to move down to London, which Rachel hated, to look for work. He was hired at last by the Prima hotel chain, and one of his first tasks was the difficult annexation of several old and proudly independent hotels in the Thames Valley. He was successful, received swift promotion, and, dividing his time now between London and Oxford, with occasional trips to Belgium, felt able to acquire the house in Oxfordshire, so much more suited, with its many rooms and its garden, to a family.

So, by that summer, Rachel's life had reached a plateau of such stability and near-boredom, pleasant enough in itself, that for all her misgivings she welcomed the news of Daniel's arrival and found herself looking forward to it. Her spirit was generous: she was willing, eager even, to believe that time had changed him for the better, and after all, she reminded herself, hadn't she also, five years before, been terrified, temperamental, casting around for a direction? How would *she* have fared if the benefit of the doubt had been withheld?

The first few days were not comfortable. Daniel was tired out from his travels and still stunned by this transplantation into alien territory. Though he did his best to conceal it he was visibly ill at ease with Karl and Megan, who for their part, too young as yet and too jovial-natured to sense his reserve, reacted to him as if he were the circus come to town, an inexhaustible source of novelty and entertainment.

Robert, understandably, was less enthusiastic. Not that he had anything against Daniel; he accepted the fact of his wife's brother with as much grace as any other aspect of her life, and there had certainly never been any conflict between the two. But his experience of Daniel was of trouble, the awful scenes at the table, the boy's destitute return from France. He recognised the marked consanguinity between the siblings, and felt somehow that Daniel represented that troublesome, buried aspect of his wife he had silently, unobserved, fought to erase. Then again, he reminded himself that he came from a large and dispersed family which had never been close, and that things were very different for Rachel. Perhaps she needed someone of her own around, especially now that he, Robert, was so often elsewhere, so tied up with his work.

Two days into his stay Daniel went down with a bad cold, and well afterwards kept to his room much of the time, emerging only at meals or when the younger children had gone to bed. Then he would join his sister, and sometimes Robert and sometimes Guy, in the dining room, fresh from the shower and all dressed up as if for an evening out, and would watch television or chat in a desultory fashion, as if killing time until the something that was bound soon to happen. He seemed more interested in the animals than in his family. At such moments Rachel felt sure she had made a terrible mistake.

Then, from one day to the next, he changed. He put aside his nervousness of the children to the extent of playing with them unsolicited, pushing Megan by the hour round the garden on her little tricycle, reading to Karl and then, when the boy's concentration waned, giving him piggy-backs through the house until Karl screamed with terrified delight. Thenceforward he did everything to integrate himself into the household. He played chess into the small hours with Robert, who loved the game and had unsuccessfully tried to teach it to both Rachel and Guy. Rachel had proved resistant because she hated games in general, while Guy was too nervy and introspective to embark on such a contest with his surrogate father. And it was over these late night chess contests that Daniel and Robert grew to know and accept each other, without conversation, without exchange of confidences, but with a sort of neutralising of any competition between them, a playing out of their suspicions where it couldn't possibly matter. With Guy, whose initial wariness had matched his own, he fell to taking long walks, ostensibly to exercise the dogs, down along the river and as far as the Old Coach House Bridge, which was Guy's favourite and private place; or he would supervise his nephew's violin pratice, taking the piano part as Guy scratched his way through a variety of numbing tunes, countering his childish frustration with encouragement, offering fulsome praise. Then in the afternoons, when Guy was at school and the younger children having their afternoon sleep, there were long conversations with Rachel; not yet the excoriating analyses of their childhood and

16

family, but a bringing up to date, a filling in of the lost years, a whole process of coming to know each other again.

He still spent much time on his own, up in his room reading, or wandering round the town or God knows where. But there was nothing secretive in his behaviour, nor indeed any lingering sign of restlessness. And though most days he still slept till lunchtime or beyond, other mornings he was up and showered long before Rachel, with coffee ready and waiting for her, and she would find him sitting with Karl at the dining table, building something in Lego or pointing out pictures in a magazine. Rachel would join them, slipping into her place, nursing her coffee, with the big dressing-gown wrapped tightly around her, for the room was cold first thing in the morning; waiting for the moment when she would feel fully awake, she was grateful for this momentary reprieve from the children's hungry attentions. 'I'll be going into town later,' Daniel would say, glancing across at her, as his sure, untrembling fingers arranged the brightly coloured blocks before Karl. 'Is there anything we need?' And their life proceeded thus pleasantly, without event, without the shadow of anything in the least remarkable, until the morning when Rachel looked out of the window and saw a strange man taking photographs of the house.

The Matter With Guy

She was carrying Megan from the bathroom when, glancing out of her bedroom window, she saw him on the pavement opposite. He was somewhere in his late twenties and dressed in a young-executive suit and tie. As she watched he took up another position between two parked cars and bent his knees slightly, searching out the most favourable angle. Puzzled, amused, and in an uncommonly friendly mood, she hoisted Megan up onto her hip and leaned through the open window. 'Can I help you?' she called down.

He was startled. He looked around at the empty street, the silent cars. When he raised his eyes and saw her his face broke into a quite charming smile. He indicated his camera as if she might have failed to notice it. 'I was taking some pictures,' he said. He had the faintest of accents.

'Yes, yes, I gathered.' She smiled back. 'Are you a tourist?'

'No, I am a businessman,' he said thoughtfully. Then: 'No, I am looking to buy. I will be coming with my business to live here, I am looking for a property. I take photographs to show to my wife, in France.'

'Well, you can't buy this house,' said Rachel. 'It's mine.' The man, his accent, his shyness on the quiet street in the fine morning, charmed her more and more.

'No, no,' he laughed, 'not this house, evidently this is impossible. It is the *type* of house, the style. I want to show to my wife, I like it very much.'

'This house? You've chosen just about the ugliest house

in the street. Why don't you look down by the river, some of the streets down there?'

He reached up to scratch his head, ruffling his rather unruly and un-executive-style hair. 'There, also, I look.'

She was in the mood for conversation, she hadn't spoken to anyone new in months. 'Wait a minute. I'll come down and make you some coffee. Then you can see the inside of the house.'

He looked about him in panic, as if, a schoolboy venturing into an ill-famed district, he had been espied and pro-positioned by one of the very women whose path he stalked. 'No, no. You are very kind, but no. I have no time. So many houses to see and pictures to take.'

She wished him luck and waved goodbye and quickly forgot all about him as she proceeded with her morning chores. Daniel slept on, his protracted convalescent sleep; it was after twelve when he appeared. Over lunch she suddenly recalled the morning's incident. When she told him of her invitation and the man's embarrassed refusal Daniel laid down his fork, frowned, and said emphatically: 'You shouldn't have done that.'

'Why ever not?'

Her astonishment seemed to irritate him. 'You don't just ask strangers into your house. He might have been anyone. Why was he taking photographs in the first place? Suppose he was a criminal, checking out the property. You don't just invite strangers into your house like that.'

'I invited you.'

He looked up, surprised, then gave a tight smile. '*Touché*,' he said.

'Come on, Daniel,' said Rachel. 'He was just a foreigner.'

'Exactly so.' He sounded quite sharp. He picked up his fork and turned his attention to the salad, spearing the green leaves of lettuce with all his concentration. She thought him troubled out of all proportion to the incident.

'There speaks the globetrotter,' said Rachel. She was annoyed, more at herself than at Daniel, for yes, of course, he was right and she had been imprudent. She had thought

19

her story might amuse him, and here he was claiming a sort of jealous monopoly on recklessness. 'It's not like you to be so priggish,' she said. He went on attacking his lunch. 'I only felt like a bit of conversation, and he looked respectable enough.'

With some solemnity Daniel said: 'They all look respectable. Only criminals can afford to dress well these days.' Then he laughed, and they dismissed the incident.

They were pleasant, those early weeks when the ice was broken, while there was still so much to talk over and Daniel's continued presence in the house had not yet become an issue. Mostly they spoke about their family, their parents, the silent atrocities perpetrated on them as children. They reverted to this inevitably, as what bound them together, the reason why the difference in age and the years of non-communication had not, after all, made them strangers. The weather was still warm, the children and animals were content with the run of the garden, and most afternoons, once Daniel finally emerged and lunch had been cleared, they would sit outside and talk or just read, savouring the unlooked-for sunshine, hauling themselves from the deck-chairs only to make huge pots of tea or change the stereo's music which filtered out over the lawns, benign, classical, reminder of an age conceivably innocent of such Freudian scenarios of buried guilts and cancerous resentments. At the same time they were astonished, even elated, to discover how similar their early lives had been, how many silent, lonely miseries had been duplicated. They unburdened themselves in the safety that neither was burdening the other, and every twist one recounted attenuated the other's old suffering and depleted its store. They were able to call up the hideous details with humour, without shame, and with a gradual lessening of that patricidal guilt instilled in them so long ago.

Which is not to say that they always agreed. In general Daniel was the more extreme in his opinions, declaring roundly and often, and as if to confirm himself in the thought, that they had both been unwanted, both been

20

unloved, by parents incapable of love. Oddly refreshing as Rachel found it, the idea carried a chill intimation of future loneliness for her: he could never bring her quite to accept it. Even so, under his prompting, she became more outspoken, found harsher terms to castigate her mother's sleepless malice, her father's vain self-absorption. The two of them entered into a tacit contest, not so much of ritual dishonouring of their father and mother, as of proving they could skewer the bugbears of the past and emerge unscathed, like children who dare each other to deny God and are not struck down by lightning. 'They're poison,' one would say; or, indulging in the luxury of feigned pity: 'I suppose we should feel sorry for them, poor old things.' Then they would giggle with exhilarated relief, causing Guy, if he was home from school, to glance up from his book in wise incomprehension of the antic ways of grownup people.

It was when they talked of their adult and separate lives that the real differences emerged. Daniel spoke of his past, Rachel always of her future. She wanted more children, she said, a whole houseful of them. Robert's present job offered stability, they could look forward to better things. This house, their first, was just a stepping-stone: she wanted eventually to move out into the real country. Or they might quit Britain altogether and set up in Belgium. The children could go to an international school in Brussels; Guy was already displaying a real aptitude for languages. Rachel would resume her aborted studies, but seriously this time: choose a vocational subject, have a career, in law maybe, or in accounting.

Daniel had no such plans. He said: 'When I get a job – when I move to London . . .' He talked remotely about becoming a waiter, or teaching French; it was as others say: 'When I win the pools . . .' Rather he spoke about his past abroad, little anecdotes of amusing local colour or which pointed up a moral. It was stories he told, and these stories were not fixed to any period of his life, but instead shimmered, polished and self-contained, freed from chronology

21

and beyond contingency: an incident in the métro, a week-end in Brittany, a description of a street at night. Even with the accumulation of these stories Rachel had no clear notion of the progress of his three years, when it was he did this job, lived in that apartment, moved to Nice or travelled to Austria. He presented his life as a guest on a talk-show might present his: little gleaming episodes, a thousand envi-able details, streetnames, cities, people. 'Once when I was at a party with Marie-Laure – ' ' – something that Gabriella said to me – ' as if defying her to ask who was Marie-Laure, who was Gabriella. Sometimes she would recognise a name from a previous conversation, and mentally assign that person a particular and relative importance in Daniel's life; but it was mere speculation on her part, and besides, names seldom recurred.

Sooner or later they would end up talking about their parents once more, indulging a conspiratorial and peculi-arly Marriner side to their characters, hitherto neglected but no less a part of their odious birthright. They rediscovered its special humour, its private language, uninhibited now by their difference in age and sex, a youth outside time. The first evening chill would send them to pursue their conversation indoors, and it was thus that Robert often found them when he returned, Rachel with her legs curled under her in one corner of the sofa and Daniel sprawled across the carpet, giddy or wistful, both of them faintly resentful of his intrusion, amused at his exclusion.

Robert might easily have become jealous at this time and developed some extreme antipathy towards Daniel, who had after all resurfaced from the nowhere of three years' almost total silence. Listening to their talk he wondered how healthy for Rachel was this incessant harping on the bad old days. But he learned, as they were all learning, that there was a whole neglected aspect to his wife which remained distinctively Marriner, in abeyance through the long consolidation of their marriage and now blossoming again like a second, and this time harmless, adolescence. If it excluded him this was only because it didn't touch him and could offer him no danger, and he took it on board as he had taken on the full mess of Rachel's life from the very beginning: her precarious moods, her child, her embattled parents. And so, acquiescing to, conspiring in, this exclusivity, he made as if to treat their daily exorcisms as a joke, feigning exasperation: 'Oh no, not your mother *again*,' he would say, finding them once more deep in conversation; or it would be 'Your poor mother, I'm almost beginning to feel sorry for her.' At such moments he was happy to take the role of some indulgent uncle who has long since put aside childish things.

'I looked out of the window this morning and saw a Frenchman taking photos of our house. He said he wanted to buy something like it. He was very charming.'

Robert said: 'You should have asked him in. Then he could have seen what these poky little hovels are really like.'

'That's what I thought. But Daniel said he was probably a master criminal.'

He came to feel a secret relief that Daniel was there. Of late he had as often as not been dead tired in the evenings, requiring only to eat his dinner and then doze in front of the television with a drink clutched in his hand. Mostly Rachel was sympathetic, venting her frustration only occasionally. But he knew he was not much of a conversationalist at the best of times, and saw that Rachel needed to talk, as a cat to hunt, to work out the stray thoughts and ideas thrown up during the day as she watched over the play of the children or flicked the pages of the newspaper.

And Daniel proved to be surprisingly good with the children. Karl and Megan were easily won over, his sheer novelty giving him automatic and irresistible allure, and after an initial hesitation he plunged quite happily into the shambolic lawless reality of the household whereby conversations were inevitably interrupted, sleep incessantly disturbed, meals always transformed into missiles.

'I want to play outside now.'

'You can't play outside, Karl, you've got no clothes on.'

23

'Well, can't I put some clothes on?'

'But I have to find some first.' She ran her fingers through the salt-and-pepper tangle of her hair, and commented: 'There's a car outside all the time, I wonder what it's doing there.'

'A car?'

'Yes, there's been a car out in the street the last few days. I didn't really notice it at first.'

'Is there anybody inside it?' asked Daniel.

'Sometimes there is, I can't really see.'

Robert stepped over to the window, looked, let the curtain fall back. 'Never seen it before.'

Guy had been listening to their conversation. 'I know that car, I saw it in town at the weekend.'

'It probably wasn't the same one, Guy.'

'It was,' he sighed. 'I know it was the same car.'

'Mummy, I want to play outside . . .'

Later, she said to Daniel with a frown: 'The car's still out there. It's making me jumpy.'

Daniel raised himself slightly from the sofa to glance out. 'Do you think we're being watched?'

'I'm beginning to wonder. There was that man the other day, taking photographs . . .'

'Don't worry,' said Daniel. 'It's probably just some old lover of mine. Or an old creditor, more likely.'

Guy was a different problem, and Daniel had been some weeks in the house before his sister confided just how much of a problem he was. His start in life had been inauspicious, his infancy difficult, divided between Rachel's lonely flat and the house, no longer suited to children, of his grandparents. But he had coped with the ascendance of Robert in their lives to the point, now, where he seemed to accept him almost as his own blood parent. The various uprootings to new towns, new homes, new schools, he had taken in his stride. Nor were there any overt signs of sibling rivalry, even though Karl and Megan appeared comparatively late on the scene, and at an age when a year's seniority is as huge as a generation's. Rachel, of course, with her habitual anguished confidence, had come to see Guy, if for no other reason than that he was the first-born, as a barometer of her fitness as a mother, so thoroughly had the idea been implanted in her brain, years before, by her mother and by the whole reproachful clan, that Guy was a problem. She came to see him as something rather less than flesh and blood, and though she fought hard against it, her notion of her own self-worth was inextricably bound up with Guy's behaviour.

So she had lived those intervening years, when Guy was doing all right, as a sort of reprieve. And now it seemed the dire prophecy was fulfilling itself. Last year she had accompanied Robert to Belgium on one of those trips of his, half-business, half-socialising. Through the protracted period of their poverty she had never been able to offer Guy a holiday, and now had the idea of taking him along.

But, far from responding to the novelty of a foreign country and this brief liberation from the younger children, he had been from the first taciturn, secretive, unusually difficult to please. He complained of stomach pains and was restless at night. They went to Bruges, ancient, once bustling, mercantile city, pronounced dead three hundred years before when the river connecting it to the sea dried up, existing still like a ghostly museum in the watery north of Europe. Guy revolted from the hushed bridges and slow canals of the Old Town, from the doorways where, miraculously preserved, the old women went on with their lace-making for all the world as if the silt had never stifled all the wealth and glory from Bruges. On one of their twilit walks after dinner he nagged and whined, pulling at his mother's sleeve and wanting to go back to the hotel. 'What's the matter with you?' Rachel demanded, irritation covering her vast disappointment: she had intended this trip for Guy, after all. One morning they visited a craft shop in the Garen-markt. The shopkeeper followed them out into the sunlight, confronted them, embarrassed: she had seen the object that Guy had secreted into his jacket. Back at the hotel Robert and Rachel uncovered a cache of other articles he had stolen during the holiday, useless things, fripperies. Guy broke down. He hadn't meant to do it, he said, he hadn't wanted to steal; but since that first evening when, leaning over the bridges of the canals of Bruges, he had met the stare of all those drowned faces, the dead faces of the people of the dead city of Bruges, inciting him to wrong-doing, it was as if he had no control over his own actions. His story, his pathetic faith in its extenuating power, bewildered and finally infuriated Robert. In the face of parental anger Guy collapsed, made himself ill with crying, and in his ensuing fever never ceased to babble his impossible story of the canals of Bruges and the faces of the dead people staring up at him. They cut short the rest of their holiday and returned to England disheartened.

But a new demon had entered their lives and taken up residence. Guy continued to steal: from shops, from his school, from his parents. He was a bad thief, unskilled at covering his tracks; it was as if he wanted to be caught. And when that happened they encountered the same tearful obstinacy: he didn't want to do it, but he had seen the dead faces again, looking into the river by the Old Coach House Bridge. When Guy's behaviour came to the attention of the teachers at his school, Rachel reached her wits' end and rashly confided everything in her mother.

'But *I* stole!' said Daniel when he learned of all this. 'When I was a child I stole all the time.'

'So did I,' said Rachel, 'didn't you know?' She looked across at him, and they sat for a moment without speaking.

Daniel stole: he had been eleven or twelve years old. He remembered the dreariness of it, the anxiety over what to do with the money, for he was not covetous by nature. He remembered being obliged to stop off on his way home from school to buy chocolate that would make him sick, or stacks of comic books that he would leave unread, or toy cars such as he had long since grown out of. One time, in a joke shop, he bought a minuscule pack of playing cards, no bigger than a matchbox, with pictures of nude women. But he didn't dare take them to school, and, having no one to show them to, felt bored with them and depressed, and pushed them to the back of a drawer.

But while the gains of his crimes brought him no satisfaction, still he stole, he couldn't stop himself, stole from his mother's handbag and from the pocket of his father's trousers while his father showered; he stole more and more, aware that he was courting discovery and impelled by this very risk. When finally Mrs Marriner discovered his cache of tawdry treasures she knew at once how he had acquired them. This did not prevent her asking him over and over where he had got the money, for the grim satisfaction of hearing him lie, cornered, squirming from untruth to ever more presposterous untruth, damning himself yet further, as if the contents of his wardrobe hiding place – the chocolate boxes, the toy lotto set, and that dismal pack of cards – were not evidence enough of his sin. Mr Marriner addressed his son in tones of deep shock; Mrs Marriner maintained an uncharacteristic silence. They did not touch on right and wrong, ignored the conventional morality of the affair. Instead it was: how could he *do* this, how could he steal from them, them, them? After all they had done? Was he *ill*? asked Mr Marriner; was he sick?

Daniel simply cried.

'It's all very well crying.'

Still he could not stop stealing. Always events followed the same pattern: the theft of the money while their attention was elsewhere, the guilty compulsion to be rid of it, then the items, whatever they were, pushed to the back of the wardrobe or stuffed under the mattress. Then the inevitable discovery, his parents' stricken expressions and lowered voices. For half a year Daniel lived in the wretchedness of his criminality, until one day, for no apparent reason, his need died. Mrs Marriner searched his room in vain.

Rachel sat with her brother in the fading afternoon and said: 'The books say – it's one of the oldest clichés – that kids aren't really stealing money from you, they're stealing what they're not getting, they're stealing affection. And, after all, it makes sense. *We* stole, when we were kids, both

27

of us. But you see, I thought I was giving Guy affection. I don't know what I did wrong. And of course, I made the mistake of telling Mother, and I asked her about the times when we were children, and we stole, and what she thought about it. And you know what she said, you know what she honestly believes? When *we* stole it was because we were bad children, greedy, dishonest, all that. But when Guy steals it's because *I've* been a bad mother to him. I can't win.'

'But you know that's not true.'

'I *believe* it's not true. But how can I ever prove it?' She turned her head and looked out through the French windows to where Karl and Megan were playing in the sloping light on the unkempt grass. 'When I married Robert, when we moved away, and then there was Karl, and then there was Megan, I really felt for a while that I was getting things right. I was doing what *I* wanted to do, I was having all these children, bringing them up the way I thought best. Maybe it was wrong of me to think like that: maybe I shouldn't have been so selfish. Maybe what I really wanted was revenge against Mother – no, not revenge, but to show her that I *could*. And maybe this business with Guy, maybe that's my punishment. Because I'll never get it back now, not even that modicum of confidence I had, when I thought I could have children and not make the same mistakes.'

Each day, Sundays excepted, Daniel would walk into the centre of the town and spend an hour or two there. Quickly adopting the ploys of the enforcedly idle he would create little tasks for himself – buying a paper, posting a letter, returning a library book – and space them out through the week, to justify these daily excursions. The spurious errand dispatched, he would walk down by the river as far as the marina, there to observe the white bobbing boats redolent of lazy wealth, or would sit for a while in one of the gracious tea shops that catered to the antique collectors, craft-market aficionados, other visitors. Passing through the narrow paved streets he could pretend that this was some old German burg, all nook and beam and Pied Piper of Hamelin. He saw few people his own age: the town lay in an established heartland of older country types and young commuter families.

He was pausing on the edge of the square one blustery afternoon when he noticed the car. Previously, through the weeks and weeks that it had stood outside his sister's house, he had paid no attention, and his comment to Rachel – some old lover, old creditor of mine – had been mere flippancy. Now, emerging into the square from one of the quaint sidestreets, seeing the car on the opposite side, no different from before and no more familiar, he was struck by an echo from the past and another occasion when he had vainly run away. He shaded his eyes and squinted myopically, but could not even make out whether there was anyone sitting inside.

His hands were trembling. He looked from side to side. The commodious country-town life continued about him, the people blithe in their respectable unconcern, and it was unthinkable that anyone might approach him, lay hands on him, here. Even so he turned on his heel, retraced his steps amongst the pedestrian alleyways, and slipped into the first near-empty pub he could find. He was scarcely able to lift his glass, so violent was the shaking of his hands, not from fear alone, but as if his whole deadened past reverberated anew within him. When the youngish barman, bored in the mid-afternoon lull, sought to engage him in conversation, Daniel, like the hunted man in a second-rate thriller, gave monosyllabic answers in a thickly disguised accent, then hid behind the sheets of his newspaper until he had finished his drink. He could not bring himself to return to the square, snatch a glance from the shadows to see if the car was still there. And, walking home down circuitous roads he had never before taken, he was conscious all the time of a reluctance to look behind him or around him: as with the unopened bills and letters from banks that once collected in

29

his drawer, he preferred to know neither the extent of his dues nor their immediacy.

His mother had called meanwhile, demanding among other things if he had a job yet, how much longer he intended to stay, what he was still doing there. Though Rachel attempted to laugh it off, though she assured him, 'You can stay here just as long as you like, just as long as it takes', it was clear that his mother's probing had had its effect. Already the projected 'few weeks' of his first buoyant return were long elapsed. He had no plans and no prospects. Even with extremest goodwill his presence in the house would from this day on be an issue. The honeymoon was over.

---- 3 ----

Work and Love

Finally, as if he could put off the moment no longer, he resolved to look up some old friends from his Cambridge days. In that first summer vacation, while Daniel in his innocence had been shoestringing it around the towns of the Loire Valley, Fran, a girl he imagined himself to be in love with, had got together with Matthew, his then best friend. There was nothing treacherous or underhand in this liaison, Fran having never given him cause to hope for anything beyond her friendship, nor Matthew any assurance that he would sacrifice his own wishes out of delicacy for Daniel's feelings. Nonetheless Daniel suffered greatly a sense of betrayal, which had the incidental effect of robbing his own summer abroad of all lingering pleasurable memory: that special day in Tours – had his friends back home known already? Had they been together? And the pair's solicitude when he returned, the tact with which they determined not to rub his nose in his own defeat, served rather to reinforce Daniel's feeling of having been plotted against: their very concern was a stratagem thought out well in advance. Naturally he came to terms with it – in Cambridge's cloistered confines this was a question of survival – and besides, he soon realised that Fran could never have been right for him. Even so this setback, echoing as it did so many of his deeper buried anxieties, left him with such a sense of unease, such a vision of appalling duplicity, as ended by befouling for him the university and student

31

life in general, and no doubt contributed to his decision, the following year, never to return.

To make matters worse, Fran's and Matthew's did not go the speedy way of most student affairs, but deepened into one of the most durable relationships that Daniel knew. Even during his periods of profoundest distraction in Paris and elsewhere he had with masochistic ruthlessness kept abreast of their story. They lived together now in one half of a house in Brixton, where Matthew was trying to finish a doctorate in musicology and Fran was an advertising consultant. The third member of the household, Saul, had also been one of their circle at Cambridge. He was teaching art to first year students in one of the London colleges, and supplemented his earnings by freelance work for various esoteric journals.

They were stupefied to hear from him and wary, but also curious, unable to believe that three years in a foreign country could not have wrought some deep change in their old troubled friend. And Daniel's departure from Cambridge was one of the great unsolved enigmas of their youth, and it is always interesting to review a contemporary so long after the event, any contemporary, even so proverbial a harbinger of bad news as Daniel. Insulated as they all now were by time and their security, they invited him for a weekend to the shabby half-a-house in Brixton, with the ecologically sound bicycles crowding out the hallway, the piles of old *Guardians* propping up the walls, the barely furnished rooms a cultivated statement of their intellectual Bohemian existence. They watched Daniel and listened to him, and found to their surprise a preternatural, eerie calm, coupled with a total reluctance to talk about himself – not prompted, apparently, by unease or embarrassment, but as if the whole past was an irrelevance.

They sprawled around on the big living-room carpet, and inevitably fell into a roll-call of former college mates. Daniel would enquire, they briefly fill him in. 'David Colling?' 'Thesis.' 'Paul Hitchin?' 'Bar school.' 'Suzanne Schaeffer?' 'She crops up from time to time in the *Independent* arts

32

pages.' Warming to the game: 'Clare Sommer?' 'Rag trade.'
'Philip Priestland?' 'Just trade.' And it was: 'Nobody knew
what became of *you*. There were the most incredible stories.'

Fran, doubtless in reaction to the lady-executive uniform
she was required each weekday to don, wore sloppy jeans
and sweaters shapeless as she could find them. Matthew
seemed as ever too smilingly massive for any room that
contained him, bear-like, clattering with panicked exclamations among the buckled old saucepans in the kitchen,
since he was the cook of the household. Saul sat languid
and long-limbed, somewhat distracted, in a Japanese robe
over his clothes. He had recently terminated a messy affair
with an older man, married. The problem was, he had terminated the affair on a point of principle, and was now
regretting it. All three of them smoked, but with a nagging
consciousness of the wrongness of the habit that compelled
them to keep the windows a penitential six inches open to
the cold autumn night.

They talked on over several bottles of a certain cheap
Bulgarian wine which was a proud badge of postgraduate
poverty in those days. At one point Matthew ventured: 'In a
way I really envy you, doing what you did. I mean, doing
exactly what you wanted.'

'Is *that* what you call it? My failure?'

'It's not failure.' This was Fran, with her newfound
asperity. But Daniel had had time enough to recognise the
widespread Cambridge misconception that it requires some
great effort of will, of revolutionary zeal, to have done precisely nothing with one's life fully three years after leaving
university.

And while his answers scarcely satisfied them they were
cautious of probing further, remembering the Daniel of old,
plangent, self-absorbed, often hysterical. They didn't ask
him overtly why he had quit the university, nor if he had
regrets, nor why he had chosen to come back to England
and at this particular moment. And, not being given to all-
night revels, by two o'clock the Brixtonians were yawning
and making noises about turning in, as if tiredness were a

collective decision, or as if they were one body that fatigue had subsumed instead of three. Daniel watched them retire with mild surprise, his wide-awake, night cat's eyes following them, blinking at them, as they gathered up the evening's debris, straightened up the newspapers, headed off to the upper regions of the house.

Next morning they had breakfast together in a local café and then wandered round Brixton Market. Their rapport was at once more superficial and easier than the night before, since Daniel could almost have been a tourist, stranger to London as he was, and they the proud hosts. Matthew bought some fish for lunch in a covered market hall which reminded Daniel of another market he had frequented, near the Faubourg Saint-Martin in Paris. Over lunch, by various references to workload, deadlines, etc, Daniel understood that perhaps he should give his friends some time to themselves, and obligingly let fall that there was some shopping to be done in the West End, and that he would be back in time for dinner. He borrowed Fran's *A to Z* and set out alone.

'What do you think? How does he seem to you?'

'Well, he certainly seems a lot more sorted out. Or is it all an act, do you think?'

'He's not giving much away, is he? What do you think he was really up to all those years?'

Or perhaps they weren't discussing him at all. Probably not: it was simply the proximity of Fran and Matthew, the best friend and the loved one. As people they were utterly unimportant to him: charming, generous, entertaining in their way, he would have liked to keep them as friends for the niceness of it, because it made him feel nice to do so. But beyond that they no longer mattered: his mind had quite left them behind, isolating instead what they represented in his life, like a silhouette which guards a human shape even as it obliterates the identity.

One incident from the afternoon was to remain in his mind long afterwards, as oddly emblematic of the weekend. He was in a pedestrian street just off Leicester Square, waiting for the time to pass. Nearby a boy of around twenty, with a pinched intense face, was jigging on his feet in the cold and staring into a window. It was not a shop window but the huge glass frontage of a sort of travel agency, perhaps the office of an airline. And it was not his own reflection nor the cardboard cut-out of a beaming air hostess that held the boy's attention, but a girl behind the desk. Looking up from her telephone call her eyes briefly met those of her attendant and she nodded, without surprise or any evident pleasure. Daniel looked at his watch: it was nearing half past five, the shops would be emptying soon, this agency would close, the girl would rejoin her boyfriend, they would go for a drink or a movie, or just home together.

Daniel turned away, overcome, and set off walking, anywhere, through the steel-grey streets. At Piccadilly Circus, around the steps of the Eros statue and in front of Barclay's Bank, a few hard-faced youths kicked their heels. To Daniel's nurtured eye they were clearly whores who still hung out in this quarter of town, if no longer in anything like the same numbers as formerly. And at the sight of them, to his astonishment, he experienced the same lurch of envy as at those lovers on their respective sides of the window at Leicester Square. These boys at least had someone to wait for, existed in relation to someone else, and in Daniel's monomaniacal vision this was all that mattered. If they were one stratum of misery above his own they were already out of reach: visible, yes, just a little way over him, close enough to talk to, their language similar enough to give the illusion that they understood him, and yet altogether out of reach. To the angels it must be a matter of indifference what circle of hell one is assigned to, but to the damned in their loneliness, how immense the difference and how terrible.

As early as Sunday morning he set off back to the relative peace of his sister's chaotic home. Short of money he hitched a lift with a youngish couple, and as they drove recalled another occasion, during that first holiday in France, when he had hitch-hiked from Paris to Toulouse.

35

The lorry driver had bade him mount into the cabin, and after some three quarters of an hour on the sweltering autoroute, had suggested they stop for beer. Daniel woke from his daydream, looked across, and saw that the man was sexually excited. 'I want to get out now,' he said, 'please stop here and let me get out now.' He was shocked – more than that: shaken – and standing alone on the grassy verge as the lorry roared off he took time to wonder why. He was nearly twenty, worldly enough and broadminded, or at least what passed for broadminded among the young people of his circle at that time. Yet whatever precocious involvements he himself might have had, it had shaken him deeply to be considered, unconsentingly, as a sexual being, to know that for *this* the driver had slowed down, for this invited him into the cabin. Penniless as he was and far from his destination, needy for help, he had not been able to think of this offered lift as anything but an act of pure and unconditional kindness, a kindness that responded only to his need and predicament, and quite different from, say, the unsolicited drink sent down the bar which one can accept or refuse. And though he hitched many times that summer and in years to come – he had no choice – he never quite recovered from this experience of betrayal, nor accepted a lift with any sense other than that of sheer necessity.

'I didn't expect you back so soon,' said Rachel. 'Did you have a good time? There was a stack of calls for you, Friday and yesterday. Robert's out with the kids, Guy's in bed. Karl will be delighted to see you, he's been missing you dreadfully. It's decaffeinated, I'm afraid, Robert bought it by mistake.'

Daniel slid gratefully into a place at the breakfast bar and watched his sister make coffee. She wore a favourite grey cardigan of his that he had been missing now for several days. It suited her. 'So that's where it got to.'

'Oh that, yes, I'm sorry. I'll get one of my own the next time I'm in Oxford.'

'It looks good on you. Who are all these people who called?'

She pushed his mug across the bar and sat down opposite him. 'I don't know, Robert took most of them. Nobody who wanted to leave a name. He told them you'd be back tonight or tomorrow morning, that's what we thought at the time. I'm sure they'll call back. You know, I really love this cardigan.'

Daniel decided at that moment to give it to her, and was about to tell her so, but taking a sip of coffee he made an involuntary exclamation of disgust.

'I know,' she said, 'it's revolting. I'll get some real tomorrow. You can't trust Robert to do the shopping on his own.' She reached for a tissue.

'You look tired.'

'The kids have had a bad couple of nights.' She shook her head. 'We're all going down with colds. Guy must have picked something up at school. That's partly why I'm so tired. Did you have a good time?'

'Are you taking anything for it, this cold?'

She frowned at him. It was the subject itself that annoyed her rather than his raising it, though he should have known better. Rachel had a deep-seated mistrust of medication and of the medical profession in general, as who would not after the two disastrous diagnoses of her youth. She preferred natural treatments when at all possible, an attitude no doubt affected by the spectacle of her parents, increasingly pill-happy with the years, never venturing forth without a full battery of medicaments, over-the-counter and prescribed, and who would have felt their numerous ailments slighted by so banal a remedy as a marjoram compress or eucalyptus inhalation.

As Rachel set about preparing lunch he went upstairs and took a long shower, luxuriating in the overheated bathroom and terribly relieved to be home after the perpetual slight chill of his friends' house in Brixton. By the time he was finished and in clean clothes Robert had returned with the sniffling younger children, and the meal was ready. Guy wandered down from his bedroom, still in pyjamas and a dressing-gown, red-nosed and forlorn. Karl was restive in his overexcitement at seeing Daniel again. Megan sat with a big grin on her face. Robert commented: 'You were in demand this weekend. I lost count of all the calls for you.'

'The car's gone, though,' said Rachel.

'The car?'

'Your rich admirer. We haven't seen it for days.'

Guy, roused from his own thoughts, said: 'No, that's not true. I saw it in town the other day, down near the Coach House Bridge.'

In addition there were two letters, both rejections from jobs Daniel had applied for. He glanced at them without interest, without emotion, inured by now to the formula. Robert waited for him to put them aside before venturing: 'If you really do want to earn some money – '

He had been applying for jobs everywhere and anywhere: in shops, offices, restaurants, locally and in London. This was the worst period yet of unemployment, as businesses closed or else had the foresight to reduce their workforce and eke out their depleted resources in hope of an upturn which never came, and the few businesses who continued to prosper could skim the cream of the dispossessed multitudes of the jobless. Daniel had no degree, his dropping out of university was like a branding of unreliability, and as he commented to Rachel when the letters of rejection first began pouring in, his three lost years were equivalent to the loss of a limb in this overcrowded marketplace.

'If you really do want to earn some money – '

He looked up at Robert, who continued, suddenly embarrassed: 'It's nothing very much, but it might give you something to do, better than the dole, until something else comes along.'

Rachel, by this stage curious, demanded impatiently:

'Robert, what are you talking about?'

'Well, I had a word with Solange, at the hotel. And they need someone to help out in the kitchen. It would only be washing up and clearing up, maybe a bit of waiting when they're short-staffed. The pay wouldn't be terrific, but at least it would be regular. I'm sure you're not interested, I wouldn't have mentioned it but for – '

'I'd love to,' Daniel said with unanswerable firmness.

'You mean, you'll give it some thought . . .?'

'I'd love to. It sounds ideal. Just the kind of thing I need. Thank you.'

Rachel meanwhile was looking at her husband, quite put out. 'Well, thanks for telling me about it,' she said with heavy sarcasm. 'You go right ahead, organise everybody's life without a word to me.'

Karl, bored at the lack of attention, had for about a minute now been singing tunelessly to himself: softly at first, then louder and with increased daring. When it was no longer possible to ignore him, they realised not only that he had hardly touched his food, but that he had been helping himself from the bread basket and crumbling the slices over the table and on the floor all around him.

'Eat your food, Karl,' said Robert, irritated by his wife's attitude.

Karl looked from one parent to the other, assessed the situation, and continued to sing.

'Karl, eat your lunch and shut up,' said Rachel.

The child did not desist altogether, but lowered his voice. Rachel turned to her brother. 'I swear to God, he's getting impossible at mealtimes. We've never had this trouble with him before.'

Daniel did not reply. He was watching, out of the corner of his eye, Karl's fingers reaching stealthily for the forbidden bread basket. When Rachel too saw it she slammed her hand down on the table, a few inches from her child, and yelled: 'Karl, if you don't stop that right now I swear to God – '

Upset by this sudden outburst of violence Megan began to wail in her chair. Karl gave in to a spasm of wildness, grasped the edge of his plate, and threw it on the floor. There was a terrible silence, broken only by Megan's uncomprehending wailing.

Robert released Megan from the straps of her high chair

and hugged her until the crying subsided. Rachel kept her terrible gaze fixed on Karl, who looked at each of them in wide-eyed apprehension, as if the plate's falling to the floor were as much a surprise to him as to anyone, then with a giggle scooped a hand over his mouth in a gesture, quite inappropriate here, that he had copied from Daniel.

Rachel still sat there, immobile, her hands grasping the corner of the table. But Daniel saw, even before her expression changed, the anger drain from her eyes, the hardness from her face: even as she looked at her son she could not keep up this severity. Allowing her shoulders to sag she broke into a rueful smile. 'Oh Karl, you're a little sod, but you do make me laugh.'

Karl sensed this release of tension and began himself to giggle. Then, cheerfully, as if improvising a catechism, he chanted: 'Yes, Karl is a little sod, and Megan's a little sod, and Guy's a little sod, and Daniel and Mummy and Daddy are little sods.'

'What can you do?' said Rachel, rising from the table to clear up the mess. 'I just can't stay angry with him, I can't help it.'

Daniel said nothing. He was trembling slightly. The incident, trivial in itself and already forgotten, had upset him, as the faintest hint of domestic friction invariably upset him, out of all proportion to its gravity. As a child he had found his parents' quarrels literally intolerable, had attempted to separate them, pleading with them to stop, which as often as not diverted their wrath towards himself. And, never having lived in a family where anger, within reason, could be healthy, or tension surmountable, he had never acquired the security to register that there are degrees in human conflict below which a household need not shatter apart. He was like a cat which, maltreated and then abandoned in infancy, will maintain its tautened instincts even in the household that rescues it, will cower at the first raised voice, panic at the least sudden movement, and flee to hide each time a door is opened; invulnerable to the idea that raised voices may be empty of menace, sharp movements expressive of mere irritation, or that doors may be opened with no more sinister intent than to let in some fresh air.

One of the waitresses at the hotel was a little Danish girl called Kristina who was effecting her six months of work experience as part of a university course in catering and hotel management back in Copenhagen. She had a smile bright and fresh as a spring morning and an air of near-prelapsarian innocence, which did not stop her giving efficient short shrift on the occasions when a male guest was moved to importune her. Then she would flee back to the kitchen, shaking her head and breathing very fast, and say: 'The fat man, he passed a comment on my bottom now.'

At another time of his life Daniel would doubtless have found her boring, unworthy of effort; during working hours he hardly noticed her at all. But it was Solange's habit, twice or three times a week, to invite the kitchen and restaurant staff for an after-hours drink in the darkened bar, to regale them with stories of her racy past and endlessly acrimonious divorce. Kristina always made a point of sitting close by Daniel, and the lion's share of her undeniably sweet smiles was clearly reserved for him. One Sunday, on their free evening, they took a train into Oxford, visited a cinema and went for a pizza over which they discussed the film. They had nothing whatsoever in common beyond their age and place of work. The next day Daniel hardly spoke to her, and Kristina suffered acute anxieties lest she had seemed over-eager. But when work was done he said, 'Let's go for a walk', and they ended up back in the anonymous room which she occupied in the hotel.

She was sweet and he grew fond of her. Sometimes they would spend the afternoon, between the shifts of lunch and dinner, on her narrow bed, and he was profoundly grateful that she seemed so disinclined to talk, to ply him with questions: or rather, so respectful of his disinclination to answer. She would lie silent across his chest as he smoked and attempted to flick the ash into an empty wine bottle on the bedside table. She was happy to go along with the idea that if words between them were few, her imperfect English was to blame.

'I wish I could tell you what you look like,' she said, 'but I don't have the vocabulary.'

'That's all right,' he said. 'I feel more at home with a girl who doesn't speak my language.'

She supposed him to have had dozens of mistresses in the exotic cities where he had lived, subscribing to a common misconception that such places impart something of their seductive power to anyone who visits them; the idea that anyone, irrespective of looks, means, assurance or lack of it, will inevitably enjoy a full and glamorous romantic life in Paris, in Nice, in Vienna, that indeed the gradations of beauty and wealth and confidence are there miraculously effaced. So she pictured to herself the succession of Daniel's women, luring him into their perfumed apartments, confiding intensely with him in midnight cafés, far cleverer, more fascinating, more skilled in the arts of love than she, and all speaking perfect English.

Solange was delighted with the young couple, and even appeared to take the credit for bringing them together, as if the fact of handing out two separate and menial jobs during a crisis of staff shortage evidenced some remarkable matchmaking intuition. Kristina came to the house one Sunday lunchtime, and though privately Rachel found her a bit dull and Dresden-shepherdess, she was relieved that Daniel would henceforth be less lonely. Robert's relief was both less personal and more so, obscurely troubled as he always had been by his brother-in-law's sexual ambivalence and concerned that no hint of notoriety should attach itself to him, via Daniel, at the hotel.

In general Rachel marvelled at her brother's powers of adjustment. It had been inconceivable to her that he should accept and appear to enjoy a job so thankless and so boring after the life he had led abroad, that he should succeed in tolerating, in cultivating the mediocre characters he was obliged to see every day after the extraordinary circle of his friends in France. And yet he did so, without complaint. From the marathons of sleep he had indulged in during those first months, he switched overnight to a schedule of early risings and exhausted returns, with only his Sundays to recuperate. He no longer dressed up of an evening as for some beachside discotheque, but was content to slop back and forth in jeans and an old T-shirt.

So she continued to be amazed at the equanimity with which he adapted to his situation. Here her mistake subsisted in the inevitable limitations of her knowledge, for if her picture of her brother's Paris life was more accurate in its particulars than was, say, Kristina's, it approached no nearer the truth. Yes, he had eaten breakfast on pavement cafés in the bright sunshine of twelve o'clock, yes, he had picnicked by moonlight on the beach at Saint Tropez. But all this – the breakfasts, the cafés, the beaches, the faces, the journeys, the nightclubs, the lights, the encounters, the nights, the nights – all this touched on her imagination unmoored from its context, the context of the life which harboured them and the mind that could flinch – that sun, that awful moonlight! – from the riches it had sought. Had she had but a glimpse of the true nature of Daniel's life, she might have understood his present contentment as akin to the grateful compliance of a rehabilitating addict, relieved to swap one dependence for another, even if that second consists of no more than the mindless tending of the hospital garden.

They spoke less. Daniel was tired when he arrived home in the evenings, and often Rachel was already in bed. He would open a can of beer and watch night-time TV and sometimes fall asleep on the sofa. When they did talk it was mostly a rehash of some previous conversation about the family, or the children, or the government.

Daniel had been working at the hotel perhaps a month when Mrs Marriner called one evening with news of their grandmother's death, quite suddenly, from a massive heart attack at the age of ninety-one. Rachel was stunned by the news and Robert, after some initial comforting, took charge of the children's bathing and bedding. This grandmother, mother of their mother, occupied an important place not so much in their lives – since Rachel saw her rarely and Daniel never – as in the family mythology which was their shared and cumbersome birthright, since Mrs Marriner had always held her up as a paragon among mothers and a repository of wisdom and rectitude. Typically this attitude had less to do with the person of their grandmother herself than with an ideal of filial piety and family duty after which Mrs Marriner hankered. This notion had trickled down into Rachel's and Daniel's respective consciousnesses, long rejected but irritatingly obdurate, like the sand one can never quite shake from a beach blanket, with the result that they had perhaps avoided their grandmother's company rather more than she deserved. Although the original of that doctrinaire puritanism inherited to varying degrees by all four of her daughters, she herself added to it the twin saving graces of humour and magnanimity, especially with age, such that in her latter years hers had come to be a benign tyranny, her edicts tempered by the wry knowledge that few were going to listen to them, none to heed them, and that the country was not going to come to its senses overnight.

'Well, better this way than any other,' Rachel conceded as she sat, red-eyed, with Daniel, who had at last returned from work. 'She hated being ill, hospitals, being taken care of . . .'

'A shame I didn't see her.'

'She never gave up on you, you know. Even when the rest of the family had all written you off, she never gave up on you. She really did think you'd amount to something.'

'I suppose we'll have to go to the funeral.'

'You don't want to?'

'Oh, it's not the funeral that bothers me, it's the thought of the get-together afterwards.'

44

'I suppose it's inevitable. Any excuse for another family knees-up.'

'Or in this case, a toes-up.'

When Robert rejoined them he found Rachel, whom he had left a short while ago in tears, giggling uncontrollably with her brother. For all the relief he felt, his wife continued to puzzle him, his wife: the mother of his children.

That night, just as Daniel was falling asleep, Megan began crying in the next room. Far from being disturbed by it he found the noise oddly comforting and restful, knowing from what sure, fixed and earthly cause those tears came: cold, wetness, hunger; knowing that in a few moments his sister would come down the dark passageway and soothe the child and then they could all sleep till morning. It was a comfort to imagine the child's cries as his own, and his own the imminent solace that would still them.

4

Memory, Loss

Luc Braillon was standing by the check–in desk of Nice's International Airport, fanning himself with his plane ticket. In front of him, leaning over the counter, a middle-aged English couple were attempting to get somewhere with the airline receptionist. 'My wife – ' the man enunciated, 'my wife – ' pointing at the lady beside him as if he were a teacher introducing a new common noun, 'can my wife have a window seat?'

'There are no window seats left,' said the girl.

'It doesn't matter, Frank,' said the wife through her teeth.

The husband glared at the boarding passes. 'Are we sitting together, at least?'

'I'm sorry, we have a block booking,' said the girl, already peering beyond the man's shoulder to locate the next passenger, which was Luc. 'There are plenty of seats in non-smoking. Or perhaps you can exchange with someone in the cabin.'

Luc gave her a sweet conspiratorial smile as he approached the desk; she did not return it. Still smiling he muttered 'Dyke' under his breath. The girl said: 'Smoking or non-smoking?' He looked around him. 'Non-smoking,' he said.

Between the check-in desk and the cabin Luc established eye contact with a girl in casual couture wear, with the father of a family, with a customs official, and with one of the stewardesses. In the cabin he took *Libération* and the *International Herald Tribune*. He was seated on the aisle, next to two English sportsmen who were carrying on a conversation of shouted hilarity with their team-mates in the row ahead. Taking his place he gave them each one muted, respectful *'Bonjour'* which they acknowledged with the faintest alarm. Luc waited until they were airborne before signalling to his stewardess. He gestured apologetically to his boarding card. 'Excuse me, there has been a mistake. I asked for a smoking seat and I have been given a non-smoking seat. I didn't notice until we were on the plane.'

The stewardess hesitated. 'You see, the smoking section is full,' she said.

Luc then indicated his neighbours, who were suspiciously attempting to follow the rapid exchange of French. 'I don't want to inconvenience these gentlemen,' he said. 'The check-in people made a mistake,' he gently insisted.

The girl frowned. 'There are a few seats free in Business Class,' she said. 'You won't disturb anyone there.' Luc reached for his coat.

In fact, there were only a dozen other Business Class passengers. Later, when the stewardess came round with the various classes of lunch tray, as she hesitated by Luc's seat, he reminded her: 'Really, I shouldn't be entitled to Business Class cuisine. It was a mistake.' But he extinguished his cigarette as he said it.

She smiled as she laid down the relative lavishness of the Business Class luncheon tray. 'It really makes no difference. *Bon appétit.'*

So Luc had a pleasant flight from Nice to London, enjoying a post-lunch sleep to arrive altogether relaxed and refreshed. As he left the plane with the other Business Class passengers he turned back and gave a dazzling smile and cheery wave to his two English neighbours, glumly hemmed in their seats. With lacerating sincerity he took his leave of the helpful stewardess and witnessed the phenomenon commonly represented by knees turning to water. Having just his hand luggage he went straight to Customs, sailing through the green channel with his usual nonchalance.

In all his travelling years no Customs official had ever asked to see his bags: even now, waving him through, one of them had classified him as far too healthy, handsome and ingenuous to warrant examination, while his colleague saw precisely the degree of ill-directed and law-fearing apprehension that plainly marks out an innocent traveller.

He had been provided with funds for the trip and decided to spend a part of the money straight away. There was also some money of his own which his friends in Nice knew nothing about, as well as a pair of rather weighty sapphire cufflinks, a gift which he would never wear and which might be sold in an emergency. He was constitutionally incapable of worrying about money when such a surprising amount of it had come unlooked-for in his young life. He was also prepared to work, if necessary.

He was a patron of the world's airports and never tired of the identical international boutiques, the indistinguishable luxury coffee lounges. First he bought a leather travelling-bag, smarter and slightly larger than his own. Then in swift succession, passing easily through the various stores, he selected and paid for a silk tie, a Bulgari belt, two white shirts, six pairs of fantastically coloured socks and six of boxer shorts no less arresting of hue, some toiletries, two ballpoint pens, and a magazine of a specialised nature. He stuffed the purchases into his new bag. He was of so impatient a disposition that he preferred to do his packing thus, on arrival, sooner than waste fifteen minutes beside the unbudging conveyor belt in Baggage Reclaim.

He found a taxi, a real old London cab, in front of the terminal. 'The city centre,' he said.

'Come again?' said the driver, starting up the engine.

'Piccadilly Circus,' said Luc, leaning back into the fragrant new imitation leather. The driver was not a garrulous type and left Luc free to flick through his magazine and occasionally circle some item of possible interest therein. Luc paid scant attention to the dull green fields of southern England, estimating that he could get the same thing in northern France for a fraction of the cost. It was only when they had passed the sedate semi-detached suburbs and were entering London proper that he showed any curiosity, and what he saw depressed him: the streets of laundromats, eight-till-late supermarts, tobacco newsagents, cafés – cafés they called themselves! – and everywhere the hoardings: advertisements but also governmental warnings against this, injunctions to do that. 'In Paris we manage it better,' he told himself; though in fact his national chauvinism was only skin-deep, a vacant and lazy certainty that France was naturally the finest country in the world. His stern comparison of London with Paris was simply to mollify his disappointment that the place looked so shabby and unsophisticated.

He got out at Piccadilly Circus and airily gave the driver four ten-pound notes. In Regent Street he bought two pairs of black trousers, an angora cardigan in a fashionable shade of grey, and yet another shirt, all of which went straight into the bag as he waved away a sales assistant frantically trying to persuade him into the changing cubicle.

The streets were very full; it was nearing the end of the working day. Luc hailed another taxi and directed it to Tottenham Court Road. The bar, in a dingy sidestreet lined with dustbins, was set up to look like a continental basement café. There were about a dozen customers, youngish, smart, who stirred as one to gaze in wonder first at his clothes, then at Luc himself. Even the barman, a dark boy in shorts and a white T-shirt bearing the logo of the café, and himself no stranger to admiration, was visibly moved by Luc's appearance.

The clientele retreated into their suspended conversations or their newspapers and into that sullen resentment which the apparition of stunning looks often arouses in a crowd. Only the barman, drawing the ring of Luc's beer and setting the can down on the bar, seemed shyly keen to talk.

'You an American, then?'

'French,' said Luc, dispensing the gracious magnanimity of his smile.

'I thought you were American to hear you.'

49

'French,' Luc explained. He drank his beer and smoked a cigarette and turned over the pages of his magazine. The jukebox was at his elbow. It exerted a sudden fascination for two unattached customers, a leather-clad blond boy of about twenty and an older, moustached type, who rose almost simultaneously from their seats to subject its menu of songs to their fierce scrutiny. The barman took out a small plate of salad and began eating it with a plastic fork, jigging his bare legs to the music. From time to time he would glance up at Luc, and smile as much as his chewing permitted. Luc returned the smile with deep satisfaction. He was beginning to enjoy his London.

Both parents were waiting on the platform. 'Did you have a good journey?' said Mrs Marriner. She did not wait for her daughter's answer, but went on: 'Are the little 'uns all right?' – affecting a cute Yorkshire folksiness she no doubt deemed appropriate to the pathos of the occasion. Daniel went to kiss his mother on both cheeks, but this alien and unexpected greeting startled her and their cheekbones collided painfully. She stepped back with a harried smile and said: 'Let's save the Continental bit till later, shall we?' She removed the bag from Rachel's hand and set it down in front of her husband, effectively detached Rachel from her brother, and marched her off ahead. Stunned, still rubbing his cheek, Daniel was left with his father, who nodded with wry satisfaction as if his every suspicion were confirmed. It was their first meeting in over two years.

The two parents had aged beyond those years alone. His father's windswept hair and beard had turned from a rather distinguished grey to a snowy, Old Testament white, and he moved and spoke with the creaking deliberation of a stage clergyman; while his mother's appearance had actually improved, she had grown somehow complete, defined, as if her hardened face and sharpened body, all their deceptive softness and roundness fallen away, had caught up at last with her nature.

They drove back through the streets of dark, crouching terraces. As they approached the town centre he noticed that a row of gloomy warehouses, empty even in his earliest memories, was being demolished to make way, a hoarding announced, for a supermarket complex. 'Yes,' declared his mother from the back of the car, 'you'll notice a few changes round here. Since you were last home.'

'It's beautiful,' said Daniel in a toneless voice.

'There's no need to be so sarcastic,' said his mother. 'I would have thought you could show a bit of interest, at least. I suppose it's all beneath you now.' Daniel closed his eyes, unaware that she could see him in the driver's mirror. 'Yes, go on, pull a face.'

His father was humming tunelessly as he drove, either unaware of or deliberately ignoring the tension. The better to express her mortification Mrs Marriner turned and began to interrogate Rachel about the children, whose presence today she had vetoed on the grounds that children have no place at funerals. Megan was too small, Karl too rowdy, and Guy – well, Guy was a problem, by turns and often with no discernible transition her beloved little grandson, an incipient delinquent, and the herald of a generation yet meaner, more acquisitive, depraved and godless than the last.

When Guy was smaller, before Rachel moved away and got married, Mrs Marriner had waged a peculiar war in her home with her daughter as adversary and her grandson as unwitting ally. Guy's problems, whether the result of a deep-rooted resistance to discipline or simple conformity to the universal patterns of infant conduct, proved a useful stick to beat Rachel with, and Mrs Marriner was always quick to cite as cause the absence of a father and the craven inability of his mother to refuse him anything whatsoever. If on the other hand she saw Guy engaged in that activity she mysteriously called 'behaving', she accredited this to her own influence, since she alone knew what measure of firmness the raising of a child required.

It was a punitive war she fought against Rachel, Rachel who had brought into the world and into her home an ignominious, an illegitimate child. But it was also a war of principles. Only when confronted with the infuriating reality of Guy himself did her principles sometimes founder, for the truth was that small children unnerved Mrs Marriner beyond reason. Guy, for his part, was terrified of her.

Ultimately all children, her own and her daughter's included, were required to fit in with Mrs Marriner's personal notion of Civilisation, a fond golden age which had apparently reached its zenith around the time of her tenth birthday, along with sweet rationing and the Berlin airlift, and whose tablets of stone were the old saws of Northern wisdom which her own parents had substituted for an upbringing, principles universally jettisoned during the precipitous descent into the moral Armageddon of the sixties and the onset of child psychology. Rachel guessed that her mother had plenty to say concerning the dangerous course on which they were bound with Karl and Megan. What perhaps held her back from saying it was a fear, not unjustified, that Robert might tell her to shut up. Mrs Marriner was wary of her son-in-law.

Now Mrs Marriner was talking about her own mother's last hours. 'A blessing it was all so sudden,' she said. 'She hated illness, she hated hospitals.' Then, to Daniel: 'Although it was a shame she never had a chance to see you, one last time. She would have liked that. She never forgot you.' (There was the faintest of stresses on both pronouns.) 'She always asked after you, you know.'

Daniel said, more irritably than was called for: 'There was no way of telling. There was no sign. I thought she was going to live forever. She showed every sign of intending to.'

The car swung into the drive. In the garden of the adjacent house the neighbours' four young children were playing. Mrs Marriner was engaged in a feud with these neighbours, and now, safe in her drive, she paused to glare at the children. 'Another one on the way, apparently,' she then observed, proceeding to her own front door. 'Catholics of course.'

Catholics served for the Marriners many of the functions which Jews had served for other generations in other parts of the country. Mr Marriner had been educated by the Catholics until he left the Church at the age of sixteen; since when, in addition to preaching the ills of their system, he had joined his wife in detecting a sort of Catholic Mafia infiltrating the hierarchy and securing top jobs for their Own in local administration, for all the world as if the appointment of an Assistant Headmaster in a small South Yorkshire town might somehow fulfil long-nursed and sinister ambitions in Rome.

Once inside she set about preparing some tea for them all, while Daniel wandered through the rooms of the ground floor. Nothing much had changed: the chairs had been reupholstered, a few ornaments had been added. Even so he felt quite unfamiliar. The house looked, smelt, like an old person's house. It was difficult to imagine these rooms had ever contained a family, children: embroidered mats on tables that had ever been displaced, polished wood surfaces ever marked by any laying on of hands. Daniel wondered if his parents' willed and premature ageing had emptied these rooms of all their vital past, or if it was some fault or dysfunction of his own memory that had swallowed the years he had lived there.

Mr Marriner sat down in an armchair and stared at the blank television screen. The silence endured. Daniel felt a rising panic. Finally he said: 'That television's new. And you've got a video.'

'Oh yes,' said his father. 'It's proving very useful.' His father then asked: 'So. How does it feel to be back in England? Not too much of a disappointment after your continental adventures, I trust?'

Mrs Marriner came in with a tray, Rachel following. Daniel picked up a set of silver coasters from the coffee table and made to distribute them. 'Ah – not those, love,' said

53

Mrs Marriner, 'they're for best.' The priority was to discuss arrangements for the next day. About the funeral his mother was calm, to the point, quite dignified. She was taking it better than he had expected. Daniel wondered if there was not, amidst the grief, a sense of liberation at the old woman's passing, for she had been a formidable presence over her four daughters and their respective families, venerated in old age as an icon rather than loved as a human being.

Dinner was served at the big table in the dining room, notorious for killing all conversation. When they talked it was about the food, so many dead compliments and dutiful reassurances, and even here Daniel strayed onto unsafe ground. At one point, as his plate was laid down in front of him, he said: 'What, no fatted calf?' – with a choked, nervy laugh. His mother set down her glass sharply on the table, and did not smile or speak for some minutes. Rachel attempted to lighten the atmosphere with a few stories about the latest escapades of the children, but her parents were loath to relax.

'That reminds me, Daniel,' said his father, 'there was a telephone call for you about a week ago. A foreign gentleman. He didn't leave a name. I gave him Rachel's number.'

'Who in the world would call me here?'

'Well, love, it *is* your home,' said Mrs Marriner.

'What a quaint notion,' Daniel said with horrid cheerfulness.

His mother's face puckered. Rachel looked at them. Why are they so cruel to each other? she wondered. Daniel was wearing a tight smile, looking down at the food he turned over and over with his fork. She had not seen him so tense in all the weeks since his return.

Sometime after dinner they found themselves alone for a moment in the kitchen. 'Well?' said Rachel.

Daniel closed his eyes. 'I don't know if I can stand it.'

She watched him, amused. 'Lighten up,' she whispered. 'You don't make it any easier for yourself, you know.' They went to join their parents for coffee. There the discussion came round inevitably to the long-running feud between the Marriners and their neighbours, and whether or not a lawsuit should be brought. The affair had begun long before Daniel's arrival in England and he was vague as to the details: when asked, Rachel had dismissed it as 'something to do with the width of a piece of string'. Apparently the Marriners felt, and felt deeply, that their rights as residents had been infringed, and they were girding themselves to do battle.

Mrs Marriner waxed most indignant as she invoked the trespasses against her. 'We can't just sit back and let ourselves be trampled on. There's a principle involved.'

'Principles can be very expensive,' said Rachel. 'If it comes to court – '

'We've been put to enormous inconvenience, this business has disrupted our sleep, even your father's health has been affected. Hasn't it, love?'

Standing firm on their islet of principle they found themselves, however, increasingly isolated. The other residents of the street whom they zealously petitioned had seemed unable or unwilling to recognise the magnitude of the outrage, while in the past few weeks the family solicitor had failed to return two phone calls, had missed one appointment, and was increasingly hard to locate. Far from intimating to Mrs Marriner that the world simply could not judge their dispute as pre-eminently important, such reactions rather reinforced her already poor opinion of craven humanity in general and the legal profession in particular. While as yet there had been no divine intervention in the matter, it was reasonable to suppose that had a host of archangels materialised in the garden to caution the path of compromise, Mrs Marriner would have written off God as a wishy-washy liberal, a self-appointed expert, a do-gooder. 'We've always tried to do right by people, we're not greedy grabbers like that pair next door. We're only defending our rights. Nothing would give me greater satisfaction than to see them squirming in court. It's a question of principle,' concluded the sounding brass, the tinkling cymbal, from its armchair.

The conversation careered on to politics, dangerous waters as of old. Now it was Mr Marriner's turn to rail against his children. He was so accustomed to his authority as a sort of unchallenged *éminence grise* in his tiny coterie that he could no longer tolerate the slightest dissent: it afflicted his vanity and rattled the torpor of his daily existence. 'The opposition front bench!' he said savagely – 'the opposition front bench . . .' He was particularly offended by Daniel's anti-government stance, giving his son to understand that by electing to live abroad for three years he had forfeited all right to an opinion on things British. 'Unemployment!' he repeated with a sneer. 'So much sanctimonious cant . . . where are your figures . . . newspapers like the *Guardian* . . . you swan back into this country, and when no one hands you a decent job within the first five minutes you start prating on . . . arrogant, dismissive, contemptuous . . .' It was a fairly typical evening in the Marriner household, and in one sense at least the prodigal could truly say he was greeted as if he had never been away.

'We're putting you in the spare bedroom,' said Mrs Marriner, as she moved about the room plumping her cushions back into normality, 'because the roof leaks in your old room.'

Daniel stopped on his way to the door. 'Oh,' he said.

His mother gave a small sigh of infinite patience. 'Well, if you'd prefer to be rained on all night long . . . Besides, we moved all your father's old junk in there.'

'I see. Well. Good night.'

The parents went off to bed and the children sat on either side of the kitchen table, drinking coffee. They looked at each other for a moment before collapsing into a kind of exhausted hysteria. When at last they calmed down Rachel wiped her eyes and Daniel said: 'God, Rachel, are we really going home tomorrow?'

'You don't help matters, you really don't,' she said. She reached across for one of his cigarettes. 'Do you think they've actually gone to bed? They could be sitting up somewhere, listening to every word we're saying.'

Daniel said: 'They've given up smoking, did you notice?'

'They're making me take it up again.' She drew deeply on her cigarette. 'You know, whenever I'm in this house, I'm sixteen years old again, and you're a whiney brat with National Health glasses and a brace on your teeth.'

'When *I'm* in this house,' Daniel said solemnly, 'I'm an eternal fifteen years old and you are a blot on the 'scutcheon.'

She giggled again. 'We're both of us disgraces to the family.'

'I feel tired,' said Daniel. 'They wear me out.'

'I wish Robert was here.' They were silent for a moment. 'It's really when I come here that I realise how much I need him. Oh, I know, I criticise him, and I snap at him sometimes, and he *is* stubborn, and infuriating, and I wish he was at home more. But one thing I have to say for him, through all the time we've been married: he's loyal. There's never been a moment when I doubted that he was on my side. The way he is with Guy: Guy couldn't ask for a better father. There was never any question about it.' She drew deeply on the cigarette. 'And it's when I'm here, with them, that I realise how important it is.'

As Daniel reached the first landing his mother appeared, in the doorway of his parents' room, wearing her white Victorian nightgown. He hesitated for a moment, looking at the various closed doors along the passageway. His mother regarded him quizzically, her head on one side, then said in a little-girl voice: 'Surely you haven't forgotten where to go?' He shook his head, but in truth he was no longer sure, standing there at the top of the stairs, under his mother's gaze, in his old home.

The next morning, after breakfast, he went up to his former room in the attic, with not the least idea of what he expected to find there. He recalled any number of films and stories where sons returned home after the wanderings of years to find their childhood rooms in shrine-like preservation, the favourite stuffed toy grinning in its corner or the train set laid out as of old, even the bedcovers turned down just the way they once were. At first glance his room was altogether as it had been, except for the large brown stain over one corner of the ceiling, and the quantities of his father's junk which had overflowed from the lumber room. A thick layer of dust lay over everything. It was very cold. On the bedside table was the book he must have been reading the last time he spent a night in this house. He lifted it, disclosing a perfect white oblong in the dust. Inside, a curlicued hand quite unlike his own gave his name and the data – *Cambridge, summer 1988*. Similar legends were to be found in the other books along the shelves, their arrangement a guide to his changing enthusiasms. Likewise a case of LPs beside the wardrobe, exaggeratedly historical, since who bought records these days?

He found a biscuit tin full of letters and cards which he opened briefly and then put aside. In the drawers of his desk were the diaries and address books from Cambridge and earlier. Many of the names meant nothing to him now: for instance, a Clare with whom he apparently breakfasted one winter Sunday morning in his first university year might have been any of three or four Clares he was friendly with at the time. *10 a.m., breakfast, Clare,* he had written with blind certainty four years ago. He made a real effort, passing in mental review the various Clares he had known. Then he remembered that there is a college in Cambridge called Clare, that the diary entry could have referred to a place as easily as to a girl. He had known several people in Clare College.

His mother was calling him from below. He took the tin of letters and about half a dozen books and dropped them off with his luggage in the spare room. His sister and parents were waiting in the kitchen, his mother very tense now that the hour of the funeral pressed on them. She looked him up and down. 'I didn't know you had a black tie,' she said.

'I bought it for another funeral, in France.'

'That's a very fancy watch you've got there.'

'I had it yesterday,' he said.

'I did notice,' she said. Obediently he held out his wrist. 'Raymond Weil, Geneva,' she read. 'Very fancy. It must have been expensive.'

'It was a present,' said Daniel. 'From a lady.'

'They're paying you now, are they?' said Mrs Marriner, with an attempt at a laugh. Then: 'We're late.'

They drove across town to his grandmother's house, where many of the family and friends were already assembled. His parents went into the kitchen to confer with Mrs Marriner's sisters, while he and Rachel ventured into a crowded room which so far as he could recall had never had any particular designation but which was quite definitely a parlour. A great number of old and middle-aged people were seated on chairs set around the walls. Daniel was able to place several uncles and great-aunts and cousins; other faces, nodding and smiling at him, were naggingly familiar; still others, friends of his grand-mother's last years, or the new spouses or friends of his many cousins, he had never seen before. He was unsure if he should introduce himself, if it was appropriate to strike up new acquaintances on such a solemn occasion. Nor did he know how to greet those he knew, if he should exchange handshakes of manly fortitude with the uncles, embrace the aunts, whatever. He watched to see what others were doing, and so remembered the etiquette of that famed northern warmth which consists in never touching anyone, however close the tie of love that binds one to them.

A jaunty voice behind him said: 'Hello stranger!' He turned and saw a girl in her mid-twenties with a tired and tear-blotched face. Then he recognised his cousin Miranda, married and mother to a baby boy. She had flown down only this morning from the Hebrides where she worked in a tourist office. Now that someone had taken the step of actually addressing him, there was a general murmured acknowledgement and one or two audible greetings. An elderly lady sitting very upright turned to him in her armchair. She was holding up a plate with a single chocolate biscuit on it and he wondered if she was offering it to him. She said: 'You'll have come a long way, then.' He smiled and said: 'Yes, quite far.' He had absolutely no idea who she was nor how she came to be addressing him with such twinkling knowledge. Then she looked away pointedly, and, following her eyes, he saw his own self smiling broadly out of a silver-framed photograph, taken on his graduation from school, that occupied a place of honour on the heavy dresser. 'You see? I recognised you at once,' said the unknown lady. And he realised that in one sense he had carried on a life here in this town, in the head-shaking, tongue-clicking affection of his grandmother, had been introduced to newcomers, had provided conversation for strangers in the form of progress bulletins and speculations about his future, all the time he believed he had vanished away in France.

Aunt Berenice manoeuvred past him with an industrial-sized teapot. 'So you're back from Paris then. It was Paris, wasn't it?'

'Yes, it was.'

'Your Uncle Sam had his wallet pinched on the Champs-Elysées,' she said.

'It's a notorious area,' said Daniel, who had heard the story before, but his aunt was already out of earshot, the spout of her teapot bearing down on some new arrival.

Then it was time to make their way out to the waiting motorcade: the hearse, the four limousines for members of the near family and favoured friends. They stood around the front door, waiting for the signal from the undertaker's assistant to release them, in groups of seven, down the gravel path to the respective cars: the daughters and their husbands to the first, then the grandchildren, then the spouses of the grandchildren and the two great-grandsons of mourning age, and finally the closest friends from the many generations of the late woman's long life. Seven people to each car: Daniel wondered if their numbers had been calculated in advance, or if some miraculous chance had elected and privileged exactly twenty-eight people in their grief. He took his place beside his sister in the hushed, plush interior of the second car. The seats faced each other, as in a London taxi. Opposite, one of his girl cousins began to cry and Rachel reached across with a paper handkerchief.

It was a long process, as several of the mourners with the rear cars were aged and unsteady of movement. His grandmother, in life the oldest of them all, had been spared this infirmity. When at last the cars eased forward Daniel was amazed at the quiet of the engines, then, thinking about it, not so surprised at all. The passengers did not speak. Ahead, beneath many beautiful floral tributes, in a white oak veneer coffin of a cleanliness next to godliness, his grandmother lay. She had died in time. Daniel looked at his sister and his cousins, reunited here and yet each summoning, he supposed, their own private memories. The dead woman had been an important part of their lives: how could it be otherwise, given the great age she had attained and the benign matriarchy she had established? Death raises some memories unbidden and requires that others be called forth, so that grief should be a difficult and ennobling thing. Daniel shut his eyes and reached down into himself, but nothing came. What he recalled were facts only: that he had last spent Christmas with his grandmother five years before, that she had sent him twenty pounds when he won his place at university, that she did not always remove her hat when she came home from chapel. But these were all things that had been commented on since, and it was the comments he now remembered rather than the events, with as little immediacy as if remembering that the Treaty of Trianon was signed in 1920, or that litmus paper turns red in the presence of acid. Of his grandmother nothing remained beyond the facts that he knew. And as he watched Rachel and his cousins with a feeling not unlike the panic of detachment he had felt up in his old bedroom,

61

he experienced the devastating totality of his loss, and knew it was this loss he should be mourning.

The service was quite short and surprisingly ungloomy for a Methodist chapel, conducted by a youngish minister. He had a bad cold; Daniel suspected that certain sections of the service had been abbreviated in consequence. Aunt Berenice was very impressed and invited him back to her house for tea, but he could not stay long, and departed pleading his ailment.

Now a palpable relief set in. The bereaved daughters were surprised at their own newfound buoyancy as they shuttled back and forth between the kitchen and Aunt Berenice's dining room, laying out plates and cutlery, adding dishes of *vol-au-vents* and chocolate gateau to the already sumptuous feast spread out along the dining-table, which had been extended for the occasion. Daniel's mother was in charge of dispensing tea, of which all gratefully partook on arrival, but there was a further relaxation of mood when Uncle Sam announced that in preference to a second cup what he really fancied was a beer, and several other guests decided they were equal to a glass of sherry, now that the minister had gone.

Daniel sat at a small table in one corner of the room, hemmed in by chairs, and Rachel went to fetch him some food. Uncle Sam slipped into a seat beside him and, wearing that jovial, bibulous smile without which he was seldom to be seen, began to recount the story of how his wallet had been swiped in Paris years before, understandably his most potent memory of that great city. 'Ah,' said Aunt Berenice, floating into their vicinity, 'he's telling you about his wallet. The first thing your grandmother said when we heard you'd gone off to Paris: "Well, he'd better watch his wallet over there." '

'Well, I never had any problems,' said Daniel.

' "He'd better watch his wallet over there",' Aunt Berenice repeated, 'I remember it clear as yesterday.'

His sister had been waylaid at the table by another aunt, Margaret. Rachel had always been much better at handling family occasions than he, at least since the stigma of unmarried motherhood had faded and she was able to volunteer anodyne news about children, home, and Robert's work, subjects more apt to inspire indulgence in their relatives than were the pernicious morals of foreign capitals, or the still more loaded question of what Daniel intended to do with his life. He caught her eye and made a desperate gesture. At that moment his mother passed by with some napkins. She gave him a tense smile and said: 'Your Aunt Berenice says, and could you tell Rachel as well, that if you want to smoke, could you go outside, at least until there aren't so many people?'

'Don't worry,' said Daniel, 'I'm going to eat something first.' Then he wondered over his mother's words: 'and could you tell Rachel as well', since no one was supposed to know that Rachel was smoking again. He felt suddenly very hungry, and the second glass of sherry had affected him in an altogether unfamiliar way. He turned to his cousin Esther and mindlessly asked a question about her job in a local government department. Esther was recently married and doing very well for herself. She and her husband had bought a house nearby which they had done up and were going to sell once the property market picked up again. She was two years Daniel's junior.

Rachel was returning with his plate. There was an eruption of laughter nearby: Aunt Berenice and two ladies he didn't know were exchanging anecdotes about his great-aunt Madeleine and her experiences during a Mediterranean cruise. Daniel remembered that he hadn't seen Aunt Madeleine today. He leaned forward the better to catch their conversation.

Next thing he knew, he was sitting on the edge of the bathtub with Rachel kneeling before him. She was holding up a full tumbler of water. 'Drink this,' she said.

'Oh no, no.' He tried to brush her away. He was conscious of the door standing open, and voices beyond it.

'Drink it.' He took the glass. Some of the water slapped onto the tiles, he looked down at it and felt a sudden wave of nausea. 'Not too quickly.' He drank. As he did so the lines of the room tilted alarmingly. Peach tiles, peach plaster, peach towels. The bathroom was unfamiliar; the situation, not.

His aunt entered. Rachel was saying: 'He'll be all right, he just needs to lie down for a while.' Turning back to Daniel: 'Can you stand up?'

Daniel rose to his feet. The dizziness swept over him, worse when he closed his eyes. His centre of gravity lurched and was momentarily lost. His aunt and sister took hold of him, one on each side, led him through the house, and laid him down to sleep in the spare bedroom.

As soon as they had said their goodbyes, his mother strode off in the direction of the car. He ran to catch up with her. 'Look, I'm sorry,' he said.

She walked away from him round to the passenger door, and stood there, pressing the handle. She stared at him for several seconds. Only when Rachel and Mr Marriner had joined them did she at last speak. 'I'm sorry, too, Daniel,' she said. 'I'm very sorry. I'm sorry about lots of things.'

Mr Marriner opened up the car and said: 'We're going straight to the station, then?' His wife ignored him, pulled at her gloves.

For the duration of the journey no one spoke.

At the station the parents purchased platform tickets and accompanied their children through the barrier. Daniel attempted to keep pace with his mother. He felt desperate. 'Look, I've said I'm sorry – '

She rounded on him. 'And that makes it all right, does it? *Sorry*? You humiliate me in front of my whole family . . .'

'I don't understand. I only had a couple of glasses of sherry.'

'A couple of glasses of sherry,' she repeated. 'You were helping yourself all afternoon, as soon as the drinks came out. You must have had at least a dozen. Everyone noticed it.'

'Then I humiliated myself. If anyone.'

'What are they going to think of *me*?' she demanded. 'What opinion are they going to have of me now? That I didn't even bother to tell my own children?'

'Tell them the truth,' said Daniel. 'Tell them I forgot. Tell them I was drunk, anything you like. Tell them I wasn't thinking.'

'No,' she muttered, 'you weren't thinking. Your grand-mother's funeral, and you weren't thinking.' She came right up to him and spoke into his face: he watched her flickering, unstillable pupils. 'Why should I have to justify myself to my own family?'

'Well, why should you?' There was silence for a moment. Then, sulkily, since the damage was done: 'Why are you so *afraid* of what they think?'

In a low voice she said: 'I shan't forget this, Daniel.'

'I'm sure you won't.'

'No. I won't.'

'I believe you.' The bars at the level crossing were low-ered into their place. Mr Marriner ventured a plea that they at least try to part on an amicable note. His wife flashed him a look of contempt but agreed to proffer her cheek for her son to kiss, closing those eyes, never still, as she did so. Daniel made one last attempt at an apology and his mother gave him a trembling-lipped, tight little nod. Then she turned to hug her daughter. The children climbed onto the train and Rachel lowered the window. She said she would call them soon.

When they were seated Rachel said: 'She thinks you did it deliberately. To embarrass her.'

Daniel said: 'She's mad. I just forgot.'

'You're not meant to forget. In our family you don't forget anything.'

_____ 5 _____

Children at Rest

The weather had turned with a vengeance during the train journey home. Robert's car was waiting in the rainy night. Karl and Megan were being overjoyed in the back seat. 'Well? How was it?'

Rachel sighed. 'We lived. We had the usual row about politics. Aunt Berenice told the story about Uncle Sam's wallet. Miranda's going to have another baby. Daniel made a gaffe at the bunfight after the funeral. He asked how Auntie Mads was.'

'And how is Auntie Mads?' asked Robert. He was in one of his sudden inexplicable jovial moods.

'Fine. Except she's been dead for a year and a half. Daniel apparently forgot. Mother blubbed.'

'Your family,' Robert chuckled. 'How can anyone be expected to keep track? Daniel, there were four phone calls for you. None of them left a name.'

'Why is it always like this?' said Daniel. 'Why do I have to go away for anyone to call me?'

Robert was pulling out of the car park. He waited to complete this manoeuvre before continuing. 'And Kristina called about tonight. I'm dropping you off at the hotel.'

Daniel had forgotten about Kristina and about this appointment. 'No, don't. I'll call her and put her off. I'm too tired to see anyone tonight.' He was anxious to be back home and in his room, to go through all those old letters in peace. More pressingly, he wanted to take a shower.

'I think you'd better go,' said Robert. 'Solange wants to see you too.'

'Solange? Can't it wait till tomorrow?'

And: 'How was Guy?' asked Rachel, in a lower voice, and in that shorthand they used for talking about Guy, since what she meant was: has he done anything else? has it started again? or some such question.

They left Daniel outside the hotel. Solange was sitting behind the desk when he walked in. 'You're wet,' she observed. 'Is it raining, dear? Listen, don't run away without saying goodnight. Your friend is waiting for you through in the bar.' He understood her to mean Kristina, though it was odd that Solange should choose the words 'your friend' to designate her own employee. Odd, too, Solange's conspiratorial smile, Robert's teasing reluctance to be drawn. He went through to the otherwise deserted bar and found his girlfriend sitting at a table with Luc Braillon. They were deep in conversation.

Luc Braillon was by way of being his best friend in Paris. They had met in a strobe-lit bar one night when Daniel was dangerously bored and down on his luck, and he had quite submissively agreed to be swept off by his new acquaintance for a barnbreaking month on the Côte d'Azur. Luc was at the time dividing himself between the capital and the south according as his rich friends desired or tired of his company. As these friends were for the most part a good deal older than himself and wary of the adolescent frolics to which he was given, he had been growing steadily lonelier for companionship of his own age and was happy for a time to add Daniel to his personal luggage, which otherwise consisted of twenty-four carat gifts and heaps of hastily packed designer clothes.

At the sight of him here in the hotel all Daniel's boredom and dissatisfaction slipped away, and expectant promise, suspended these last months, flooded into their place. And yet, he asked himself, why should Luc cause him such emotion? Had he really been so bored, so dissatisfied, that Luc's appearance should operate this kind of chemical disclosure, exposing this want of glamour in his life? Luc was guaranteed to upset the precarious equilibrium he had established, the humdrum sobriety of dishes and children; capricious, catlike in his allegiances, utterly undependable, Luc was also the kind of person who, after being the life and soul of the party, might wake up a friend at four in the morning, sobbing and incoherent down the phone, complaining that no one loved him, no one understood him, that he was quite alone. In Daniel Luc inspired exhilaration and depression by such rapid turns as left him winded, for he emulated Luc at the risk of earning his contempt, played sidekick at the risk of irritating him by his submission, held aloof at the risk of being labelled a spoilsport, struck out desperately on his own only to be told, shatteringly: 'That's just not funny.' And in all this Luc acted entirely without malice, for he had a genuine love of Daniel and – Daniel's sole trump card – a vague yen for him so long established as to have become a joke between them. It was simply that Luc was one of those individuals, common enough in the world, whose anger outweighs their loyalty. Thus the occasional strain or hiccup in their relations could be brushed aside by Luc as of momentary consequence even as it assumed apocalyptic proportions for Daniel. To cite one typical but memorable instance, Daniel had suffered and sweated for days following a riotous party that Riviera summer when he had persisted, high on the Luc-elation as he was, in attempts to drag his friend into a giggling ring of dancers, only to be told: 'You're drunk. You're boring. Go away.' It was at least six months before Daniel found the courage to allude to that evening: genuinely baffled, 'What party?' Luc had responded. 'What dancers?'

Finally, to round off the syndrome of emotions brought on by Luc, Daniel felt the first little tug of jealousy. As he moved forward between the tables Kristina looked up, broke into a smile, pushed back her chair in readiness to greet him. Luc sat there looking like an advertisement for himself. There was not time to explore which one of them he felt jealous of; simply to register the familiar pang followed by the dull ache he invariably experienced when two friends of his, previously unknown to each other, came together.

He kissed Kristina, slightly longer than usual. Then he turned to the French boy. 'Christ, Luc. What are you doing here?'

'Can we stick to English so that Kristina understands?' said Luc. 'And is that any way to greet an old friend who's come all this way just to see you?'

Daniel sat down. He glanced quickly from the one to the other, gauging the extent of their intimacy. 'So you two have got to know each other then,' he redundantly said. 'But Luc, how did you find me?'

Luc indicated the tiny black notebook lying in front of him, a little telephone book. Now he picked it up and dangled it in front of Daniel's face. 'You really should know better than to leave this kind of incriminating evidence lying around. Can't you even leave the country properly?'

Daniel made a grab for his notebook. 'Where was it?'

Luc shrugged. 'It was lying round at Saskia's place. I guess she didn't even know what it was. I called up a friend of yours, nice guy, name of Saul. He gave me your number, didn't have your address, I guess you never gave it him. But he said you were working in some hotel. So, when I called three times and still nobody was home I took a bus up here. Second hotel I walked into, asked at the desk, they told me you'd gone up to see your folks. Hey, Daniel, I was awful sorry to hear about your granny.' He dropped his hand on Daniel's.

'Forget it,' Daniel said lightly.

'Was it awful?'

Daniel felt suddenly uncomfortable, here in the hotel. 'Listen, can we possibly go to a pub or something? This place is dead of an evening. And Solange doesn't normally like staff drinking in here.'

'Solange is the lady out in the lobby?' Luc asked, with that unmistakable distracted interest of one who already knows the answer. 'Well, sure, fine by me. Kristina?'

Kristina had been waiting, politely, for an opportunity to speak. 'Oh, you know,' she said, 'I think I will be going. I'm so tired!' She performed a little pantomime of sleep. 'It is a good possibility for me to get some sleep, maybe. And you two will have so much to talk about. I see you tomorrow, Daniel, is it okay?' She was already standing, collecting up her bag, her coat, with a slight smile as if uncertain of having done what was expected of her.

Daniel looked up at her, then across at Luc. He detected conspiracy and in spite of himself was impressed by Luc's efficient handling of the situation. At the same time he felt cheated of his moment with Kristina, deprived of being able to take her aside, of appealing to her discretion, tactfully but firmly, as he invoked a glamorous Parisian past, old ties, exclusive masculine collusion. Ignoring Luc for a moment he walked her out into the corridor. 'You're sure about this?' She nodded. He put his arms round her. 'I missed you.'

Her little eyes were bright. 'I missed you too. Go and talk to Solange now.'

Luc joined him in reception. Solange gave the French boy an adoring look. Has he won over the whole hotel already? Daniel wondered. Kristina, Solange – who next? 'Darling Daniel, can you help me?' pleaded the manageress. 'Ernst has done a bunk.' Ernst was a waiter who had joined them the previous week, since when he had sustained two fits of hysteria in the kitchen and made an unsuccessful pass at Kristina. 'I say good riddance, actually,' Solange drawled on, gazing piteously at her rings, 'but it does leave me in rather a hole. Could you possibly save your poor old mother's life, darling? You'd get paid a hell of a lot more than for washing up, naturally.'

'I've never done waiting before,' said Daniel.

'Darling, it's the job you were born for. And let's face it, you had no experience washing up, either, when you started. Please say yes, darling. You'll look so lovely in your little uniform. Tomorrow morning, ten a.m., all right?'

When they were outside Daniel said, buttoning his coat

and looking down at his fingers as he did so: 'You asked Kristina to leave us alone, didn't you?'

Luc only smiled broadly, and said: 'A smart girl, she is. She could work it out for herself.'

It was beginning to rain again. As they walked to the pub Luc explained that he had spent the night in the hotel, had actually taken a room there: 'not up to my usual standards, of course, but they do a nice breakfast. Actually,' he went on, 'actually I was wondering if I could crash at your place tonight. You know, I've completely run out of money.'

There was an experimental note to this admission, and to Daniel, reminding himself that money had never been a problem for Luc nor a concern, had never altered the pattern of his life one iota, this 'I've completely run out of money' sounded like a lie or an irrelevance. But still he said yes, of course, there would be no problem for tonight.

They pushed open the pub door and a violent gust of wet wind swept with them into the bar. A group of boys, toughly got-up and unsmiling, turned to stare at them – or rather at Luc, since it was he who commanded their attention. Another young man, clearly of the same gang, had just paid for some drinks at the bar, and was lifting two brimming pints of lager as they entered. He set them down again sharply on the counter and looked at the arrivals. Daniel whispered: 'I don't know if this is our sort of place.'

'Oh, I know this pub,' Luc said with satisfaction. 'I was here last night.'

It was certainly obvious that the pub knew him. As he swept forward to the bar the landlord gave him a nod of unenthusiastic recognition, and the bearer of the drinks was seen to rejoin his friends in their hushed conferral around the pool table, with their many sharp glances towards Daniel and Luc.

'What were you *doing* here last night?' asked Daniel as they waited for their drinks.

'Relax,' said Luc with supreme confidence. 'Why should we fear these locals?'

All the same he selected a table at the far end of the bar,

away from the youths and their stares, and even this proved to be a less than inspired precaution, since they were sitting just next to the lavatories, and the succeeding twenty minutes witnessed an unlikely incidence of brief calls paid by the members of the pool table crowd.

Daniel did his best to ignore all this attention. He lifted his glass to toast Luc. 'It *is* good to see you again.'

Luc was staring at his upraised wrist: 'Hey, Danny, nice watch you got there. Not a present from Saskia, by any chance?'

'How did you know?'

Luc grinned. 'Saskia shows a stunning lack of originality in her choice of gifts. So, Danny, tell me: you serious about this girl?'

Daniel laughed, delighted. 'You don't have to say "girl" with quite that note of contempt.'

'You serious about her or what?'

'Kristina? She's sweet. We get on. No. I'm not serious about Kristina.'

'So, Danny.' He plucked at the billows of his silk shirt, examined his cuffs. Then he leaned back and narrowed his eyes against his friend. 'So what's it all about?'

'What's what all about?'

'This. England. Look around you, Danny.'

Daniel did so, obedient, not even irritated. 'Do you mind?' he said, and helped himself to one of Luc's cigarettes. He took his time lighting it. 'I had to get away,' he said at last. 'And this is fine. I hardly drink, I don't take anything anymore, I get nine hours of sleep, minimum, every night. I eat three meals a day. I read. You know? I'm actually reading books again.' Luc began to say something. 'No, wait a minute. There's Kristina. It's not much, not serious, not yet, all right, I admit that. But there are the kids too, Rachel and the children. It's something new to me. A family. All the family I've got. It may not be terribly exciting, but just at the moment it's all I want.'

Luc was smiling broadly. 'No, seriously, Danny. I wasn't

accusing you of anything back there. I was curious, that's all.'

Daniel inclined his head slightly.

'Just one question though. If you're so settled and cosy, how come you were so pleased to see me and so ready to dump Kristina tonight?'

'But Luc,' said Daniel. 'But Luc, I love you. Really I do. You're a – you're a friend.' The word felt uncomfortable. He had almost said 'mate'. 'I wasn't rejecting anything, not you, any of you, Paris, anything. I just had to move on.'

'Move back.'

'Move on.'

Luc patted him on the hand. Then he stood up. 'Come on, I'm going to get us some more of this.' He twisted his empty glass in the light. 'These Brit measures. You might as well inhale it.'

First he went off to the lavatory. Alone, Daniel became aware of the chill once more and of the group of ever-curious youths on the other side of the bar. One of them smiled across at him and batted his eyelashes in exaggerated mockery. Daniel looked away. The boy called over in mincing tones: 'I like your friend.' When Luc returned with the drinks another of the boys shouted after him: 'Hey.'

Daniel said: 'Look, can I pay for this? You said you were short of money.'

Luc was scornful. 'I'm all right. Don't worry about *me*.' Animated with enthusiasm, he said: 'What you were saying back there, I was thinking. Maybe I wouldn't mind sticking around here for a while myself. Country life. Anonymity. Nothing's spoiling in France. I can give it a break. What you think?'

Daniel said: 'You mean here? In England?'

Luc spread his palms wide. 'Why not? I speak the language. I can do any old kind of work, doesn't matter how boring, how little they pay . . .'

Daniel suddenly understood what Luc was leading up to and just how thought-out this apparently spontaneous idea had been. He suddenly felt the weight of Luc, his proximity,

73

his will to get what he wanted. He took a gulp of the drink Luc had set down before him. 'What would you do? Where would you go? London?'

'London – ' His gesture was dismissive. 'I don't know anyone in London. Listen. You got this new job as a waiter, right? So that means, your old job in the kitchen must be going free. They'll need someone straightaway.'

'But Luc – ' Daniel tried to laugh. 'It's an awful job.'

'You were happy enough with it yourself.'

And as Luc outlined their immediate strategy – how they would go together tomorrow to the hotel, approach Solange, try to secure staff accommodation 'just till I can get an apartment, a room' – as the pure force of his will overrode all objections, Daniel's initial panic gave way to resignation, and with it came the thought that it needn't be such a bad thing to have Luc around for a while, that Luc might well provide exactly what was lacking in his life. And then he began to wonder why he had felt so threatened by the idea a moment ago, and so instinctively resistant, when Luc was such a good friend and so amusing and had travelled all this way to be with him, after and in spite of his own ungracious departure. And then he felt he should make amends to Luc, whose intentions were so very good. He leaned across and punched him lightly on the shoulder; he laughed. 'Staff accommodation. Did you put this idea to Kristina, by any chance?'

Luc grinned, blithe at being found out. 'It came up in conversation, sure.'

One of the pool table crowd, a short boy in army fatigues, called over. 'Hey, you back there.'

Then, with Luc's future mapped out and Daniel's too, they fell to talking over Paris and old friends. Daniel's disappearance had caused quite a stir; telephone lines had burnt late into the night between Paris and the Côte d'Azur. He was puzzled to hear it, and this overlaid his natural gratification. The glamour and edge of a world where lives and fortunes might be shifted, be wholly redirected or even withdrawn as a consequence of the sudden departure of one little English tourist who had vastly prolonged his holiday – all this he found too difficult to square with the circumscriptions of his own life now, divided as it was between his sister's house and the kitchen of a country hotel. He could not remember why he had been so important, why his bit-player's status had been so grandiosely upgraded. But Luc made a good story of it all; and Daniel had to allow for a degree of exaggeration.

They had slipped into French at some point in the conversation, perhaps in unconscious reaction to one of the youths who, passing their table on his way to the Gents', had slowed his pace quite markedly. The alcohol and the pleasure of the old language smoothed their inhibitions somewhat, and their conspiratorial exchanges gave way to louder chatter, more strident laughter. The boy in the army fatigues set down his drink, gave an angry sigh as if provoked beyond all reasonable endurance, and approached their table. He glared down at Luc and said, in a voice surprisingly soft: 'Hey, Frenchy. You're having such a good time. How'd you like to suck my cock?'

Luc continued to talk, as though nothing untoward had happened. And it occurred to Daniel that he might actually not have heard, that he was not simply ignoring the boy at all. He recalled that Luc was almost deaf in one ear – he always forgot which one – his eardrum shattered in the course of some adolescent discipline administered by an enraged stepfather or equivalent. And the boy had spoken quite softly, as if uncomfortable with the grossness he had been required to deliver. But if this were the case, if Luc had failed to hear the boy's insulting question, what was Daniel to do? He could hardly interrupt his friend, say: Luc, the gentleman is addressing you. On the edge of his vision he noticed that the boy's companions had shifted nearer, apelike spectators, to watch developments.

Luc reached for his glass, and the hand of the boy in army fatigues clamped down on his wrist. Daniel saw his friend's eyes narrow a fraction. In the silence Daniel began to tremble, slightly sick at the inevitability of violence, now that the incident had slipped the confines of the rules and conventions of a public place, the presence of impartial witnesses. And after all, he knew quite well that violence did occur, that fights did break out in pubs and bars and that people were hurt. Luc was now staring at the hand that gripped his wrist. The boy said: 'Hey. I was talking to you.'

Somehow Luc freed his hand from the boy's grasp. He seized his glass and smashed it, there in the centre of the table. He leapt to his feet, trembling, his face white and contorted, a torrent of really foul language pouring from his mouth, of which Daniel could catch only isolated words here and there: *'Putain ... fils de pute ... saleté de fils de pute ...'* There was some dreadful old Marseillais slang mixed in there, but even without this it would have been impossible to understand him, so shrill was his spitting voice. His aggressor was stunned, he stared open-mouthed, while Luc, now in tears with his rage, stood and screamed out his invective. Daniel had wondered for a moment if this were not some act, some ploy to wriggle out of physical confrontation. But it wasn't an act, for Luc continued way beyond reason, and his friend was reminded of nothing so much as a cat which, cornered, will with its claws, its teeth, most of all with its sheer unblinking terror, inflict appalling damage on the humans who could easily have crushed it. Suddenly the ranting stopped, he stood for a second speechless, his lower lip quivering, then he swept the remaining glasses and ashtrays from the table, gave a strangled sob and fled, unhindered, out of the bar, the door crashing shut behind him.

There was a silence. All were staring at the space so recently occupied by Luc. Then, slowly, their eyes turned on Daniel. The boy in army fatigues, the one who had started it all, attempted a laugh. 'Your mate, he's fucking off his trolley.' Facing their stares Daniel began to fear for his own safety, but by now the landlord had emerged from behind his counter, was looming over towards him. 'Outside,' he said.

Daniel cast around for his jacket. Luc had left his coat,

too, and his bag. The upturned table lay beside him, the spilled drinks seeping into the carpet. He began: 'Look, do you want me to give you a hand . . ?'

'Just get outside.'

'It really wasn't our fault, you know,' he said. The landlord leaned against the door, huge and uncompromising, his arms crossed over his chest as if to indicate that the rights and wrongs were of no interest to him.

'Do yourself a favour,' he said. 'Don't come back in here, you and your friend. You two on holiday, right? You can surely find some other place to go amuse yourselves.'

'I live here,' said Daniel. His teeth were already chattering with the cold rain that blew in from the street.

'There are places round here, you know,' said the landlord on a kindlier note. 'You just have to know where to look.' He sighed. 'Your friend. He was in here last night. You can't imagine what he was up to.'

Daniel turned, wretched, his arms full of Luc's coat, Luc's bag. 'I'm sorry,' he said.

'Son, you know,' said the landlord, almost fatherly now, 'I don't think he's normal.'

There was no sign of Luc in the street outside. Daniel stood in front of the pub for a moment, looking at the swimming pavement. The shock of this latest drama finally hit him, and he realised he was trembling from something other than the cold, while in his arms he felt the weight of Luc's bag, his coat, the whole awful weight of responsibility once more. He swung the bag over one shoulder and set off down the street, into the night's violence. He had no idea where to look, no idea what way his friend, deranged as he had been, might have headed off. Did Luc even know his address? An icy raindrop inched, miserably, down his collar. He trudged up to a crossroads and watched the streaming cars, then crossed over.

He was halfway down the opposite side of the street when a hand reached out from nowhere and held onto his arm. 'Danny.' He swung round, steadied himself against the wall. He was breathing very hard. Luc stepped out of the doorway of an office supplies shop and gazed into his face.

'Danny. Hey, Danny. Don't cry. Look, I'm sorry, I scared you? I gave you a scare back there?' Daniel was weeping quite uncontrollably now, his whole body was shaking. Helpless, Luc bit his lip, cursed himself under his breath, then: 'Hey,' he said, 'Danny, here, I got a present for you. Give me that bag. I got a present for you, I picked it up in London. I was going to give it to you later, but now – hell, Danny, please don't cry, I can't bear it.' He lifted up the present. It was a black scarf, really quite beautiful, with the words *Emporio Armani* embroidered in white. Luc had gone shopping in the Brompton Road, and now most of his clothes bore the logo of *Emporio Armani*.

'Put it round you, you're cold,' said Luc, passing the scarf around Daniel's neck himself and smoothing it across his chest, like a mother dressing her favourite son. 'There. That's better. You'll feel better in a moment. Come on, now. Can't have you crying away in the street like some old girl. Oh God.' The wind tugged jealously at the scarf. Luc put an arm round Daniel's shoulder, led him, unresisting, to the edge of the road, and, though no plan had been formally announced for the remainder of their first evening together, and though ostensibly he had no idea where Daniel lived, said: 'Come on now, I'm taking you home.'

The walk and the rain calmed him down and camouflaged his crying. He called cheerily through to the living room: 'We're here!'

Robert was watching a made-for-TV drama. Rachel already wore her dressing-gown; she sat nursing a mug of hot chocolate, the excuse for which had been provided by the recent deterioration in the weather. As they entered she stood up. 'This is Luc,' Daniel announced, 'a very very great friend of mine from Paris. He's come all this way just to see me. Can he stay here tonight? Only tonight?'

She looked across at Robert, who reluctantly lowered the volume. Then she said: 'Yes. Yes, I don't see why not. Of course. Does he – ?'

'I speak English, yes,' said Luc, stepping suddenly forward to give her his extravagant greeting. They sat him down and Robert made up a drink and put it into his hand. Rachel apologised for her state of undress and Luc assured her that any apology due was his. 'Daniel suggested that I come here tonight, I would have been quite happy to spend another night in the hotel.'

Daniel said: 'He spent last night at the Old Coach House, I mean he actually took a room there.'

Robert looked up at this. 'Really? And what did you think?'

'Robert handled the Old Coach House takeover,' Daniel explained, 'when it became part of the new chain.'

Luc, whose terms of comparison included among very many others the Beverley Wilshire and the Venice Cipriani, invariably at someone else's invitation and expense, lifted his glass and said: 'They made me very comfortable.'

'You'll be roughing it here, I'm afraid,' said Rachel. To Daniel: 'I'll just go and make up a bed in the spare room.'

'That's all right,' said Daniel, 'don't bother. I'll sort it out, thanks. I know where everything is.'

Luc excused himself to use the bathroom. As he disappeared down the hall Rachel burst out laughing. 'He kissed my hand!' she said in disbelief. 'I don't think anyone's ever done that to me before. The thing is, it would have been sickening from anyone else.'

'But not from him, right?' said Robert, visibly less impressed. And it was a general rule that men cared less for Luc, unless they were men who cared very much indeed.

More thoughtfully Rachel said: 'He's very good-looking.'

'Isn't he, though,' said Daniel, with all his secret pride.

When Luc returned they pressed him to have another Scotch, but the boys had picked up a bottle of wine on the walk home. They took a couple of glasses and a corkscrew and went upstairs. At the head of the staircase Luc tilted his head inquiringly towards one of the closed doors. 'No,' whispered Daniel, 'that's Guy's room,' and Luc nodded approvingly at this information.

They listened to some music, very low. Daniel lay flat on his bed, the wine balanced on his chest. Luc sat cross-legged on the floor, his hair shielding his face and his head bent as if over an invisible guitar. 'Luc, tell me honestly. Did you come all this way just to get me back?'

'I'm on holiday,' Luc protested.

'No, but seriously.'

He was silent, deliberating his words. Then he looked straight up, as serious as Daniel could wish. 'I didn't see why you should think you could just up and leave as easy as that. But no. I'm not here to get you back. I wanted to see you. See what you were doing here. What you were trying to prove.' He made an expansive gesture: the room, the monastic bed, the wild Oxfordshire night.

'Nothing. I'm trying to prove nothing.' Daniel stared up at the ceiling and remained quiet: there was a section of the music he was listening for. When it had passed he said: 'Let's go to London.'

'London? When?'

'Some time. You're such a fan of London. Let's take a few days. We can stay with some friends of mine – Saul, the guy you spoke to. We can go out, take in a few clubs. It would be fun to do that with you.'

They talked on into the night, luxuriously, making plans realistic and fabulous. Only when the wine was finished and Daniel suddenly very tired did he hark back to his earlier question and mention the name which had not been spoken all evening.

'So Carlos didn't send you after me?'

Luc said: 'Would I tell you if he had? Look, I'm on holiday. Besides, I thought the whole business with Carlos was over.'

'It is.' Then, more decided: 'Of course it is. I'm here, he's there, of course it's over.'

'Of course it is,' Luc echoed with scorn.

Daniel sat up, looked at his friend with real affection. 'Thank you for the scarf.' He yawned and covered his eyes with one hand. 'I'd better get some sleep.'

They both became very still. Then, as many times in the past, Luc reached across and brushed his fingers over Daniel's leg. He said softly: 'So, Danny: how about it?'

Daniel looked down in puzzlement at the hand, then turned to his friend with a pained smile, as many times before. 'Now, now, Luc,' he admonished gently. 'This is my sister's house. And what about Kristina?'

So, turning their backs on each other, they stripped to their underwear and then turned off the light. And that night they slept, scarcely touching, scarcely moving, side by side in the narrow bed, like two sons of a poor family.

—— 6 ——

Faces of the Dead

So the next day, quite early, Daniel took Luc along to the hotel for a chat with Solange. The interview went something like this:

'What kind of work have you done before?'

'I worked for two years in a fairground.'

'Lovely. Where was this?'

'Well, all over France, really. Mainly the south.'

'And what were you doing, dear?'

'A bit of everything.'

Solange repeated tonelessly, as if making notes: 'A bit – of everything. All over. For two years.'

'Well, I took the money from the kids, operated the rides, that kind of thing. I did the – what do you call it? When you throw a ring, and if it lands on something . . .'

'Hoopla,' provided Daniel.

'I see. Two years. Well! And did you like the job?'

'It was great. Travelling around, you know. The owners were drunks. An old couple. You could always cream off a fair bit for yourself, they'd never notice.' He laughed.

Daniel raised his eyes heavenward. Solange said: 'I see. Now, dear. Have you ever done any serving?'

'Oh yeah. At the fairground again.'

'And what was that?'

Momentarily Luc was at a loss. He looked to Daniel for help. *'Barbe-à-papa,'* he said, 'I've forgotten what it is in English.'

'Candy-floss,' obliged Daniel.

82

'But this job isn't serving, is it?' Luc asked hastily. 'It's washing dishes, right?'

Solange said: 'We can never be sure what might come up, dear. It's useful to know.' But in any case the result of the interview was a foregone conclusion, and Luc was hired and allowed to move immediately into the staff quarters. 'We can dispense with formalities,' Solange said. 'Daniel, darling, you take him round, introduce him to everyone.'

So Luc went to live in his small back room and began his new job. To his credit he worked hard, never complained of being bored or tired, and maintained a charming good mood with the staff in the kitchen. Most days he joined Daniel and Kristina for the post-lunch lunch provided by the hotel, then the three of them would repair to another, cheaper hotel down by the river, for a beer or, in Kristina's case, a coffee. Sometimes they went for a stroll past the boat-moorings, or browsed in such riverside antique-shops and booksellers as had not yet been driven out of business. They rarely met up at the end of a working day, since Luc finished well after the pubs' closing-time and Daniel was reluctant to hang around late in the hotel bar. After that first night, in fact, apart from hurried cigarette breaks in the kitchen garden, the two boys were hardly ever alone together.

It was the next day that Kristina had asked: 'What does he do, your friend Luc?'

'Just what you see him doing. He moves around and makes friends.'

'He's very confident, I think. Maybe too confident. I cannot think that you two have so much in common.'

They were lying in her room, with nothing more strenuous to do than watch the afternoon fade beyond the curtains. Daniel looked with delight at her intensely-dieted form. She crossed her arms on his chest and laid her blonde head on her arms. 'We don't have much in common,' he said. 'That's the secret of our friendship.' He laughed. 'I mean, I sometimes think he's a psychopath or something.'

Kristina, to whom the word 'psychopath' was not familiar, said: 'He's gorgeous. Does he not like girls at all?'

It pleased him, the anonymity of her room, so banal and functional, so different from the anonymity of hotel rooms he had stayed in, arriving in cities he didn't know, rooms full of promises and anxieties. He did not answer but watched his cigarette smoke curl upwards to the low ceiling.

And Guy had mentioned, thoughtfully, to Rachel: 'That boy who was here this morning, with Daniel. I've seen him before.'

'Are you sure?' said Rachel. 'He's only just arrived in England.'

'It was him all right. Just yesterday, maybe the day before. Down by the bridge. He was standing there.'

Daniel could not remember why he had been so upset in the pub that evening, why he had felt so threatened by Luc's insurgent presence. After all, he had witnessed, had courted far worse violence in Paris and elsewhere, falling asleep in his subsidised finery on the stairs of underworld nightclubs, provoking drunken arguments with utter strangers in cut-throat dives, lurching home from yellow lamp to yellow lamp down low-life streets at four o'clock in the morning, so peacock-clad and incapable as to present a positive incitement to attack. Was it that he now cherished his life, his physical well-being, in a way he hadn't before? For all his propagandising to Luc he could not feel that he had so much more now to lose than in the old days, in Paris.

His new job waiting at table was a good deal more tiring. What free time remained he spent at home, watching tele-vision or playing with the children. Rachel was already missing those heady early weeks of her brother's idleness, the interchangeable afternoons of luxurious talk. She had acquired the habit of his exclusive company and its absence left her feeling lonely.

She had other concerns. Robert was being pressed to accept a post in Brussels in the new year. Unquestionably it would be the best thing for his career; for the family, for Rachel, for any eventual hopes she had of returning to work or further training, the advantages were less certain. She had not much liked Brussels.

Robert simply dropped the whole matter one evening into her lap. 'It's your decision,' he said. 'I'll be happy to do whatever you choose.'

She didn't welcome this responsibility; rather, she resented it. 'What if I don't want to decide? What if I don't want to choose?'

Then there was her mother on the telephone. 'I don't understand you. No sooner are you settled in one place than you want to upset it all and start up somewhere else.'

'Nothing's decided yet.'

'I wish you'd get yourself sorted out. It's always been the same with you. And what's your brother going to do?' Since the incident at the funeral she avoided referring to Daniel by name.

'He's still at the hotel, still looking for a job in London.'

'Of course it *has* to be London. Is he helping at least?'

'He doesn't have much time, with his work.'

'Work. Washing up in a hotel.'

'He's not washing up any more. They made him a waiter—' Even as she spoke she regretted it. Why should I be made to feel defensive? 'Anyway,' she said, 'he *does* help. He's very good with Guy.'

'Guy? But Guy doesn't need any looking after. What is he doing with Guy?'

One afternoon Rachel returned from shopping with Karl and Megan to hear music from the dining room. Guy was at the piano; it was a piece she had never heard him playing before. She stood in the hallway for a moment, hushing the children with her stillness, listening to the unfamiliar and quite difficult music, Guy's ferocious concentration. Stepping closer she peered through the slightly open door, and saw Guy bent over the keyboard, and beside him, tall, taller and ganglier than usual, it seemed, his body arching over the boy, his concentration fixed on the back of his nephew's head, engaged in some unnameable communion, was Daniel. Suddenly he looked up at her, and simultaneously

Guy broke off playing, like the mechanical coordination of a single body. She smiled nervously at them and withdrew, herding Karl and Megan through into the living room, closing the door behind her. Guy resumed playing, but it was a familiar piece and an easier one. A few moments later Daniel wandered in. Deliberately casual she asked about the music, what it was, how Guy came to be playing it. 'I don't remember Guy learning that one,' she said.

'Oh—' Daniel was moving about the room, restless. 'Oh, it was just something we dug up from the bottom of the piano stool. I was just giving him some help.' In the background Guy had moved onto some scales.

'It sounded good,' said Rachel. 'No, I mean it. You two should work together more often.'

'Oh no,' said Daniel with a smile. 'It was just to keep Guy company.'

She was busier than ever with the younger children; Karl in particular demanded near-constant supervision. Rachel supposed that Guy was in need of company. Meanwhile the question of Belgium loomed over the household, and she guessed that Guy had cast her as villain alongside her husband for even considering the possibility. Guy made no secret of his feelings, which were unfair but understandable, and if the subject arose in conversation he would get up abruptly and leave the room, and then have to be coaxed back with treats or promises. He was more truculent than usual with Robert. On the other hand, if several days elapsed with no mention of it, he would ask suspiciously: 'So, are we going to Belgium or aren't we?' He had lost all interest in learning French and no longer tried out his infant vocabulary on Daniel.

Belgium was ineradicably associated in all their minds with Guy's problem. Until only a few months ago they had spoken of 'that business in Belgium' to refer to Guy's apprehension in the gift shop in Bruges, as they stepped from its interior out into the pavement sunlight – 'Excuse me, madam, was your son intending to pay for this?' Belgium, with all its associations, acquired a dire magical significance, as if the very iteration of its name might break the charm and release the demon once more. She knew this was superstition. She grew angry at herself, at the immediacy of the choice that faced them, at Robert whose career made this choice necessary, at her lack of faith in Guy and at the bequest of guilt down the generations of her family.

'He was late home from school again on Tuesday,' she said. 'I couldn't get a straight answer from him.' They were sitting in the kitchen; Guy was out at his violin lesson. The next day Daniel was away with Luc for the long-awaited weekend in London: they had been saving up their days and half-days from the hotel.

'It probably makes things worse if he feels you're watching him all the time,' Daniel observed from behind a newspaper. 'It's the same with ex-alcoholics. You can push them back onto it by thinking about it too much. I heard about it on a documentary.'

She was not in a mood to be reassured, was irritated by his airy certainty. She thought: he sits there in my kitchen, spooning yoghurt into his mouth... She began moving around the kitchen, opening cupboards, pulling drawers. 'Twenty to seven. Robert's not back. I should be starting dinner. Somebody has to go and collect Guy, we have to pay his teacher.' Running her fingers through her hair she looked about her in quiet despair, as if the kitchen constituted a reproach in its very disposition.

Daniel marked the page and closed his book. 'I'll go,' he said. 'You stay here and deal with supper.'

'Would you mind? I'll write you out a cheque, you can give it to his teacher.'

It was quite dark, the dark of an evening at the end of the year with only the streetlamps and the lights of curtained living rooms. Other people's houses were comforting in their warmth and exclusivity, their privacy and protection: the arm that draws the curtain enfolds the progeny. Even outside and at this remove Daniel could take comfort from it, as from the knowledge that out here in the cold and dark he was about much the same business, family business, venturing forth to bring home the last child and see him safe to bed.

He dispatched his business with the teacher and took hold of Guy's violin. 'Turn your collar up,' he instructed Guy, 'it's cold outside.' Guy glanced up at him before obeying. It was odd the way Guy trusted him: warily, always after a moment's consideration, as if making a conscious decision to do so.

He was humming and smiling to himself. Guy's voice broke in on his thoughts. 'Well? Have they said anything more about Belgium?'

'I don't know, Guy. I don't think anything's been settled yet.'

Guy began to walk a little slower. Clearly he had something on his mind. At last he said: 'I don't want to go to Belgium. That's where it all started.' He no longer risked adult anger by referring explicitly to the business of the canals in Bruges, the old story that lay behind his thieving.

Daniel said cheerily: 'Don't worry about it. I'm sure whatever Mummy decides, it'll be for the best.' They had reached the main road, and still Guy dragged his feet.

'Listen, Guy. Shall we take a different walk home? Shall we go down to the bridge and watch the river?'

Guy was looking up at him, his eyes very wide and liquid. After a second he nodded. There was still plenty of traffic on the road and Daniel reached out his free hand to take Guy's mittened paw. The boy slipped his hand up to Daniel's wrist. 'Your watch is very nice,' he said. 'I suppose it must have been very expensive.'

'I guess so, old man. You see, I didn't buy it myself. It was a present.'

'Someone must have liked you very much, to give you this watch.'

'Mm-hm,' said Daniel. 'And maybe one day when you're older someone will like you enough to give you a watch like this one.'

Guy glanced up at his face. 'They must have been very sad when you went away like that.'

'I guess they were, Guy, I guess they were.'

'Don't you think you should have given the watch back, when you came to England?'

Daniel squeezed his nephew's hand. 'It was a present, Guy. Of course not. People don't just take presents back when other people go away. Otherwise they wouldn't be presents.'

Guy appeared to consider this, but soon returned to his older preoccupation. 'You wouldn't be coming to Belgium with us, would you. I wouldn't have any *friends* there. I wouldn't be able to talk to anyone. I didn't like Bruges, it was creepy.'

'You wouldn't be going to Bruges, you'd be going to Brussels,' Daniel said, to deflect the subject. They had reached the river. 'Here we are.' They walked out onto the bridge. Guy stood on tiptoe to look down at the sluggish water. The bridge, the river, this was Guy's special place; but he had come here tonight on Daniel's whim. It was extraordinary how Guy trusted him, neglectful uncle that he had always been. Daniel moved up closer to the boy, staring at the back of his head, as if to penetrate and peel apart that animal trust. Here, only a couple of yards from the main road, yet out of the raking headlights of the cars, it would be easy to push him over. Did Guy's mind conceive such an infamous act, in the moment before he decided to trust him?

Guy's cold white face turned up to Daniel's own. He said, scarcely audible: 'You can see them too, can't you?'

Daniel laid his hand on the back of the boy's neck, between his hair and upturned collar, and felt his own coldness against the warm flesh. He gazed down at the river.

'Yes,' said Daniel, exhaling with relief. 'Yes I can. I've been able to see them for a long time. But that was in another country. And besides—' He couldn't remember what came next. He strained for a moment into the shattered archive of his memory, imperatively conscious that here was something he had once known, once understood:

until his constitutional lassitude had the better of him, and he let it go. He swallowed, shivered. 'Let's get you home.'

As they walked along, quite briskly now, Guy said in a firm young voice: 'I'm glad.' He asked: 'Will you tell Mummy, about what we saw?'

'I think Mummy's got enough to worry about at the moment, don't you?' They were approaching another crossing and Daniel took his nephew's hand, more for its warmth than for safety's sake. He told himself that he had not misled Guy. It scarcely mattered, anyway, what there was to see down there: old junk, shadows on the dark water, or the inciting faces of the dead themselves, who knows. The important thing was not to betray the child's trust. They crossed the road together.

7

Children at Play

Paid, well-rested, and innocent of the sleepless future almost upon them, the two best-turned-out young men to grace the railway network that weekend descended on Paddington in a mood of exalted hilarity. 'So you're going to show me London,' announced Luc, strutting through the crowds. As yet Daniel had been unable to ascertain quite how much of London Luc had already seen, in the three days between his arrival in England and his appearance in Oxfordshire.

'Listen, it's different with a native,' Luc insisted. 'It's more authentic.' They boarded a tube train. Luc waited until the doors had shut behind him to enquire: 'These schoolfriends of yours. What kind of friends are they?'

'Actually they're friends from Cambridge.'

'That's what I meant,' said Luc.

'They were my best friends there. We were a sort of gang.' He was staring up at the plan of the line, counting the stations still to go. 'If you must know, I used to be in love with the girl.'

'And her new guy's your old pal?'

'It was a long time ago.'

'It must have been,' murmured Luc, straphanging with some flair. He was wearing a prissy white dress shirt beneath technicolour braces which exercised a sort of hypnotism over their fellow passengers. 'Well,' Luc continued, 'I hope they're not the quiet-evening-in-around-the-library-fire type, is all, because I want to go out on the town.'

Staring back hard at a seated girl in school uniform he hooked a thumb under his braces, pulled, and let the elasticated material twang back. 'Like my braces?' he asked her in a very loud voice.

He was overexcited – irritably, childishly so, as if London were Christmas and the longed-for gifts disappointing. He strode out of Brixton Station and up the hill with no idea of where he was going, and passed loud, insolent comment on all he saw – the numbers of black people, the worthy vendors of the *Socialist Worker*, the near-uninterrupted lines of estate agents' hoardings along the main street. 'For sale: whole second floor of London,' he said with some disgust.

Nor, when they reached it, was he impressed by the cheery squalor of the Brixton house. As they followed Matthew up the stairs he turned back to Daniel and whispered: *'Tu as vu le bordel?'* Have you seen the state of this?

But he introduced himself to the three friends charmingly enough, thanked Matthew for inviting him, told Saul: 'At last. We talked already on the telephone.' Daniel noticed Fran's eyes narrow a fraction when Luc took her hand and said: 'So you're the famous Fran.' Matthew explained that he was preparing something rather complicated in the kitchen and, after pouring out a glass of wine for everybody, went off to attend to it. This caused Luc to prompt: 'What about *our* wine, Daniel?' – and Daniel to produce the bottle of Piper Heidsieck champagne from his bag, handing it over with a bashful smile.

'Champagne!' said Fran, gazing at the bottle. 'Thank you.'

'Luc's idea,' said Daniel.

He was content to sit back and let his friend be the new centre of attention. 'Yes, I came to England to visit Daniel, that was my original plan. But then I loved it so much here I decided I would stay awhile. It will help me improve my English.'

'Your English hardly sounds in need of improvement,' said Fran graciously, even though Luc was pronouncing his words in a slightly more foreign way than usual.

'You are too kind.'

She was wearing a dark green threadbare cardigan several shoulders too large, giving her a waiflike appearance as the fingers of her little hands emerged to light and then smoke a cigarette. She wore no make-up. Her hair was fantastically structured with a buttress of pins and grips and barrettes.

'You must tell us some stories about Daniel's scandalous past in Paris,' she said. 'He's so secretive about it.'

'Only if you repay the compliment,' Luc charmingly returned, 'with scandalous tales of Cambridge.' He pulled slightly at his jacket. The house was large and draughty, and the window stood, as usual, six inches open against the cold November evening.

'So, Luc – this was Saul – 'so you managed to find Danny after all.'

'Of course. Thanks to you.'

'In spite of the wrong number?'

'Wrong number?'

Daniel glanced up swiftly. Fran, too, lifted her eyes from the swirling wine in her glass, and listened with a new interest. Saul looked from one to another, aware that his innocent, banal question had acquired a sinister import between the asking and the hearing of it, but still he floundered on: 'I gave you the wrong number, it was an old number, from an old address book, I realised just after you'd hung up. I thought you might ring back but you didn't . . .'

His voice tailed off. Luc was sitting there with a rattled smile on his face, and Daniel had a sudden sickening intimation of conspiracy, the unpleasantness of deceit uncovered and the weariness of explanations required. Everyone was waiting for Luc to speak. But Daniel didn't want an explanation, he didn't want to know by what means Luc had tracked him down. An idea came to him, how he might save the situation, and he said to Saul: 'It must have been my parents' number you gave him.' And to Luc, on a note of jocular reprimand: 'You didn't tell me you spoke to my parents, Luc.'

Luc turned to face him, smiling broadly. 'That's right,' he

said. 'I completely forgot. I called your parents, and they . . . and they . . .'

'. . . and they gave you my sister's number,' Daniel finished off.

Just then Matthew appeared with more wine and stood there in the doorway, immense, grinning, the bottle in one hand and a corkscrew in the other. Fran said: 'Do you want any help, darling?' Daniel found a Velvet Underground album which had been a great favourite of theirs during the first university year. The awkward moment passed.

More talk followed and more wine until Matthew ordered them to the table. He had cooked an enormous paella which Luc exuberantly praised for all the world as if France had been some sort of gastronomic penitentiary. Daniel felt he was playing up the naïve and eccentric foreigner a bit too hard.

After dinner Matthew and Fran entwined themselves on the old couch while the others lounged over cushions spread out across the floor. They finished the wine and opened the champagne and Matthew rolled and lit a joint which was passed around, and Luc served up with merry candour various tales from his highly coloured history. 'Daniel and I? That's quite a story. We met in a bar one night, in Les Halles. Danny was absolutely drunk. I was leaving Paris the next day, early, to go stay with some rich friends of mine in the south, but Danny wouldn't let me go, he kept saying no no no no, just one more drink, one more drink. And I thought oh my God, no way I'm going to wake up in time to make this flight, so I said to him: "Why don't you come with me?" I figured as how if I could freeload off these people down south, somebody else could too. And he said okay, and we got up to go collect his stuff. I said to him: "Don't you think you'd maybe better pay for all these drinks?" And he stood there, swaying, you know, with his hands in his pockets, and said, very English: "You understand, I don't have a penny to my name." ' He laughed richly. Daniel faintly smiled.

It was clear the Brixtonians were undecided whether or

not he and Luc constituted an item, as in truth any number of sexual and emotional metamorphoses might have come in Daniel's life since the days when he was so long and so famously Fran's unrequited lover. Matthew had been visibly embarrassed when it came to explaining the night's sleeping arrangements to Daniel: 'We're making you up a bed in here and Luc can have Fran's old room, if that's okay, but if you want to change anything . . .' Daniel had smiled to himself, not dissenting, amused by the delicacy of the situation even as he felt a glow of pride at being mentally coupled with someone so gorgeously exciting as Luc, as if it were a measure of how far he had travelled since the time when they first knew him.

Here was Luc, for instance, cheerfully resurrecting his childhood and the unimaginable poverty of backstreet Marseilles, that misery which, on other nights long ago, he had poured out, with whisky and retching anger, to Daniel in the little skylit apartment in Paris. 'My mother was a drunk, I suppose she is still. Always there was some strange man about the house. My mother is too generous, she gives always too much, and always, these men, they took everything and then ran. My sisters and me, we had to pick up the pieces. Then one day – I was fourteen – one of these guys ran and he took me with him, and that was that. So it's hardly surprising I turned out the way I did. Oh, sure, sometimes I get to feeling sorry for myself, but it's not such a bad life when all's said and done.'

No doubt they took a lot of it – this unchecked prodigality of his past – as exaggeration, a camp and continental brand of old familiar macho boasting. Certainly nothing within their experience could be further removed from Fran and Matthew's liberated monogamy, nor from Saul's intense, artistic relations with intense, artistic young men. Saul, indeed, was watching the guest with half-concealed scepticism and that peculiar puritan disdain which people like Luc often and unwittingly inspire, as if stunning attractiveness were in itself a form of self-indulgence. As for Fran, she was torn between amusement at Luc's exotic lack of inhibition, and suspicion of the exclusive masculinity of the world he represented. Although no avowed feminist, she was alert to misogyny in all its forms. And while in fact Luc quite liked her, admiring her feistiness even if he did think that she dressed like a dyke, nonetheless her appraisal was fairly accurate of how little she, a mere woman, must count for in his eyes.

'It's not such a bad life, when all's said and done.'

And Fran said: 'It sounds like it could be pretty lonely. And pretty dangerous.'

Luc shrugged. 'No danger. Not when you know the rules. It's just a question of sticking to certain rules, taking certain precautions.'

'Such as?'

'Such as: never stay for breakfast. Do what you want, with whoever you want, for as long as you can, but don't ever stay for breakfast.' He lifted his glass which contained the last of the champagne. 'Cheers.'

They took a bus down the hill and then a tube to Green Park, to a jazz club favoured by Matthew. There they stayed for an hour or more, while Matthew enthused about the music and about the even better jazz he had lately heard in Hamburg, but Luc and Daniel were itchy for less sophisticated pleasures, and so they took a taxi to a riotous club in Camden Town. As they queued for entrance Matthew commented, looking about him in dismay: 'I think I'm the oldest person here.' One moment of the evening found Daniel and Fran alone for the first time in three years: Saul was valiantly trying to collect drinks at the crowded bar, while Luc and Matthew had long since disappeared onto the dancefloor. Fran said: 'Of course, you know what we're all wondering, don't you?'

Daniel feigned ignorance, and she jerked her head in the direction of the teenage throng amidst which Luc was somewhere dancing.

He said smoothly: 'But Fran, you of all people should know which way I'm made.'

'Let's say I used to know. I used to think I knew.'

Delighted, he took her by the hand and led her onto the floor. It was a joyous evening. They stayed to the closing of the disco and took an extravagant London cab home to Brixton, the five of them perched in the cabin, delirious and exhausted. As the taxi sped over the river Luc pronounced it one of the most thrilling evenings of his life.

The household began to stir some time after midday, and their varying degrees of hangover and exhaustion united them in a kind of appalled comradeship. They breakfasted from the depleted buffet of the previous night's feast, picking at bowls of cold paella and buttering little squares of toast with the duck pâté. Matthew, rubbing his eyes every half minute or so, announced that he couldn't face eating anything, and decided that just coffee was best. All three of them had work to do, they said, and would rather send their guests out to explore – and in Luc's case, shop – on their own.

The boys wandered the streets of the West End, behaving much as they had done in the good old days in Paris, loafing about the big stores like truant seminarians, standing in front of the windows of coffee-houses and making faces at the waitresses within. They shuffled into a newsagent's and at once began leafing the pages of the mildly pornographic magazines from the topmost shelf, exchanging exclamations of pubescent awe so loudly and for so long that the elderly Chinese proprietor, alarmed for his upstanding clientele, hovered out from behind his till, at which point Luc swung round and bought the cheapest pack of chewing-gum on display. Then it was out into the freezing street, hands thrust into pockets, stamping their feet from cold and aimlessness, getting in the way of shoppers already laden with Christmas parcels, watching, with the detached sadism of the young, one woman lose her step on the wet pavement and her brightly-wrapped purchases cascade into the gutter. Fran made them tea when they returned, and sat with them on the big living-room rug. 'Matthew's cooking pasta,' she said. 'Nothing very exciting, I'm afraid.'

'I wouldn't be able to eat anything exciting,' said Luc,

'after the riches of last night.' Fran paused in the act of lifting the teapot and turned her head to look at him, wary for sarcasm. He went on: 'So your boyfriend does all the cooking in the house? You certainly have him well trained.'

Fran replied with more than usual asperity: 'It's true, but I'm the one who goes out every morning to scrub the household washing down in the stream.'

'I meant no offence,' said Luc gently.

'Luc's only winding you up,' said Daniel.

'Is he? That's all right, then.' Saul entered at that moment with a bottle of wine, stood and took in the little group on the rug. 'We're having tea,' Fran told him testily.

'English tea,' said Luc. 'Unfortunately, it is past four o'clock.'

Over the pasta supper the Brixtonians announced that they would be staying home that evening. So decided were they on this point, and so profuse their good reasons, that Daniel immediately suspected them of holding a conference while he and Luc were out in the city. The suspicion made him uneasy, as if in his friends' reluctance to continue the party were an implied disapproval: of clubs, of undiluted nightlife, of Luc – by extension of himself. He urged them to change their minds, knowing from the start he would only reinforce their decision, but needlingly anxious to goad them on to furnish further reasons, further excuses. 'We really wouldn't be good company . . . can't take the pace . . . so much to *do* tomorrow . . . we'd cramp your style . . .'

'But Fran,' said Luc, lifting the bottle, filling her glass, 'but Fran, it won't be the same without you strutting your stuff on the dancefloor.'

By now Daniel was impatient to leave, but Luc, languidly and repletely sprawling across the rug, altogether as if he owned the place, insisted on one more bottle of wine and a quick game of cards. Almost inevitably, with tensions as they were, he scored an easy victory and thus further exasperated Fran, who was a notoriously bad loser. The two of them left at nine, Daniel fairly dragging his friend from the house, with no clear destination, since none of the places

98

they knew of opened before ten. In the event they chose to kill time in a French-style bar-café in St Martin's Lane, where Luc flirted outrageously with one of the waiters and Daniel compensated, as much for this new indignity as for his recent discomfort in Brixton, by drinking nearly a whole bottle of wine. 'Your girlfriend doesn't like me,' Luc commented. 'Perhaps she is jealous.'

'There's nothing between her and me, there never was.'

'It's not a precondition for jealousy. Look at you and me and this waiter. Why else do you scowl at him so?'

'Let's go,' said Daniel, not before pouring out the last dregs. Their waiter was nowhere to be seen, which fact did not perturb Luc.

'Perhaps he will join us, in the disco. He said he might, perhaps.'

Thirty minutes later, standing at the bar in the club, Daniel was already questioning the wisdom of his evening's intake of wine. For the first hour he stuck to mineral water, and remained with Luc on the edge of the immense floor, passing unstrenuous commentary on each batch of arrivals, and not dancing, for the place was as yet half-empty and Luc liked to pace himself, reserving his energies for those hours of prime excitement and exposure between two and four. Around midnight Daniel began to feel much better and at once, stupidly, got himself a gin and tonic. He was sipping at it when a favourite song of his started up, at which he drained his glass in one and pushed himself from the wall as if it were a river bank and the dancefloor the swirling river.

He and Luc were separated within seconds. His frantic energy held up for about half an hour, though he glanced out occasionally over the sea of bobbing heads for a familiar face. Then there was a longish interval where he just sat at the bar, drinking more gin, staring at his reflection in the mirror, staring at the spectral blue liquid in his glass, waiting for Luc to rejoin him. He was terrifically bored by the vast, expensive, non-event of the club, even though it was no worse, in its noisy succession of too familiar or forgettable songs, its epic cast of types, its unrelenting discomfort, than any other, and it was sheer self-delusion on his part to expect, as he never failed to do, some crescendo of thrills and crowning excitement, to feel disappointed, cheated even, when the Great Night Out disintegrated into its separate, predictable, dispiriting elements.

Long abstinence had raised his expectations, and with them the stakes of disappointment. He looked at the faces along the bar. He looked out over the dancefloor. He knew nobody. Worse, there was not even the prospect that someone he knew might come shouldering his way through the crowd. If he wanted to talk to anyone he would have to initiate contact himself. But what could he say, what original, winning words shout over this pounding music? He knew nothing of London, of the life here, of its codes. He felt suddenly no better than a provincial runaway aground in the metropolis, and all his experience and sophistication unravelled, worthless. He looked at the faces around him, then at his own pale image among the bottles in the bar mirror. No one looked as lost, as alone as he; everyone seemed either a part of some group or else intimidatingly self-sufficient, and though he knew this for an illusion, the knowledge made him feel no better. These melancholy thoughts chimed with a particular level of self-pitying gin intoxication and he saw in the mirror, before he even felt it, his face redden and pucker, saw the moisture gather in his eyes, so undiluted by time and reflection that the tears he discharged might as well have been the very alcohol he had drunk a moment before. He left the bar, climbed the stairs and found Luc, at a table in the gallery, deep in conversation.

Somehow he managed to get himself into a seat. 'Danny, hi!' said Luc with public enthusiasm. 'I think you two know each other.' Daniel rested an elbow on the table and looked closely at Luc's friend: a comb, some hair-gel, black leather trousers and a ripped T-shirt had effected a modest transformation, but this was still recognisably Luc's waiter from the Charing Cross café. 'Christ, Danny,' said Luc

100

under his breath. 'You really might have laid off a little.' Daniel helped himself from somebody's cigarette packet and sat back, elsewhere, nodding his head inopportunely and quite failing to follow the conversation which resumed, strained now, opposite him. Soon afterwards the friend got up and left. Luc rose from the table to follow, but not before 'Christ, Danny,' he said once more, with a headshake of finality.

Daniel now began to feel sentimental. A boy came to occupy the seat vacated by Luc, and Daniel bought him a drink. They chatted for a while about this and that, and though the boy's comments and answers were altogether ordinary, within minutes Daniel had decided they were going to be great friends. He leaned over and took the boy's hand, and heard himself suddenly recounting the disappointments and frustrations of the evening, heard his own voice unstoppably reciting the tedious, meaningless details. 'Don't you want to come and dance?' the boy said gently. They made their way down the staircase, Daniel with his eyes fixed on the back of his new friend's neck, for balance. He felt quite elated: his daring had paid off, he could still manage it when he tried. But as he reached the edge of the dancefloor he looked around and realised that the boy had already disappeared. Daniel saw him a few moments later, dancing and chatting with a group of friends. They returned his stare with suspicion and disapproval: it was obvious that they had been talking about him.

Now he rallied. He was not going to hang around to be gossiped about by some teenage barfly and his posey chums. Dancing had burnt off some of the drunkenness, and he resolved to seek out Luc and drag him away. He edged a way through the crowd, making a superhuman effort not to stumble against anyone or tread on anyone's feet. There was Luc in a far corner, dancing with one of the club's rare girl visitors, their movements synchronised with real skill.

Daniel yelled over the noise, 'I'm going up for air,' accompanying his words with gestures that could have meant anything. Luc turned his fixed manic disco smile and cupped a hand to his ear. Daniel leaned into his friend's perspiration zone and shouted the words once more.

'I'm coming too,' Luc shouted, 'I've had enough of this place.' He made to follow Daniel without a word or glance for his dancing partner, who froze in mid-bend and stared at Luc's vacant space with the same helpless shock as if her own reflection had turned away and departed. The two boys made slow progress up the stairs, for people were pushing their way down, a late crowd, groups of eight and ten arriving from their various parties. Daniel said: 'I had no idea this place was so popular.' Luc said: 'We got here too early.'

New arrivals crowded round the cloakroom, loading the counter with thick winter coats, scarves, bags, issuing instructions as to which item might go with what or whose, which permutation was more practical or economical, since somebody might want to leave earlier than the others but somebody else had the car keys in her bag. Among these newcomers clearly the girls were in charge, pushing past Luc and Danny, shouting over their shoulders – 'We'll be in the downstairs bar' – and leaving their boyfriends to wait in line, deposit the communal paraphernalia, and meander down after them. Luc leaned against the wall and tried to wipe some of the sweat from his forehead. 'It's like being backstage at a theatre,' he said. 'So where do we go from here?'

'Let's just get outside.'

Even when they had their coats they couldn't get out to the street, as one of the bouncers was involved in an argument with a girl who had positioned herself half-in, half-out of the door. 'You've got the wrong guy,' she kept saying, as if to an imbecile.

'I don't think so,' said the bouncer, and insultingly folded his large arms in her face.

They were tuning up for what might be a lengthy slanging match. 'Excuse me,' said Luc, 'if we could just get through.'

To let them pass the girl was obliged to step back onto the pavement, and the bouncer took advantage of this momentary retreat to slam shut the door. The girl was furious – 'Fucking frog' – then she turned away, defeated, to where her boyfriend, an emaciated old-young man with a ponytail and an air of such determined gloom as could scarcely have been lifted by any of the entertainments on offer inside, hovered and skulked between two parked cars.

The boys stood for a moment, stunned by the cold. Luc seemed to have some difficulty remembering where he was. At last he explained: 'I took something back there, in the toilets, I think it's starting to work.' Daniel slipped his arm through his friend's. 'Do you want to go on?' he said with little enthusiasm.

Luc stared at him, puzzling over the question, then gave a high-pitched laugh. 'Your face!' he managed to say through his mirth. 'You look like a kid that's just done *pipi* in his pants.' At that moment there was a roaring sound and an explosion of lights, and suddenly three motorbikes were there in the street, had pulled up, ranging themselves in a half-circle about them, engines revving wildly. In the blinding light that beamed full on them they could make out only the huge, science-fiction silhouettes of the avenging dark riders.

'Let's get out of here,' said Daniel, making to grab Luc's hand.

But one of the riders called out 'Luc! Hey, Luc!' He removed his helmet, shook out his hair, and it was the boy from the café. As if in a trance Luc moved forward into the road, to stand direct in the beam of the motorbike's light. 'Hey, Luc!' the boy shouted. 'We're going to a party, you want to come?'

Luc stood there, a black angel streaming with light. He called back to Daniel on his precipice. 'Sure! Sure I want to. What do you say, Danny? You coming with us?'

Already the bikers were revving harder and harder in their fury to be off. Daniel shouted across the few feet that separated him from Luc. 'No, no, I'll catch you later, you just go on.'

The biker who was Luc's friend lifted his powerful arms to replace his helmet. Then he reached them out and closed his hands on the handlebars. Luc, floodlit in the glare, gave a yelp of delight, swung his body over the seat, leaned his head against the huge arched back and clung tight to the boy's waist: together they resembled some mythological beast-man. '*Adios, Danny*!' he called back. Then they were gone, leaving a cloud of mephitic smoke, and the street empty.

Daniel looked about him for a moment, then down at his wrist, where his watch had been, and couldn't for the life of him remember why it wasn't there. Really shivering now, for the dancefloor sweat had turned cold and clammy, he turned back to the club entrance with no other wish than to know the hour of the night. But when the bouncer saw him standing there, his body shaking, his teeth chattering uncontrollably, he said with a heave of disgust, 'No way, not you again', and slammed the door in his face, and, though Danny held his thumb down on the bell, then beat on the door with his fist, would not open to him. 'I only want to know the time!' he shouted. He felt he might be sick at any moment.

He set off back down the street, which led to another yet quieter street, at the near end of which was only a gloomy passageway of dustbins and drainpipes and bricked-up windows. Two darkened neon signs said respectively BOOKS and STAGE DOOR. The passage smelt of urine. He halted halfway down it, for he had the sudden distinct impression, so still and dead was all on all sides, that he stood in the exact centre of the night, equidistant from the last train and the first, as far removed from the warm beery lights of closing time as from the first blear-eyed rattle of breakfast.

He emerged on a main thoroughfare which he did not recognise and whose eclectic array of banks, boutiques and burger chains gave him no orienting clue. A few people were standing at a bus stop nearby, and Daniel approached them, politely addressing a young couple seated under the shelter. 'What's the time?' he asked. They answered him, quite friendly, and he nodded and turned away, only to realise a few seconds later that he hadn't heard their reply at all. Embarrassed, he moved off to scrutinise the bus time-table. At the words Tottenham Court Road a ray of hope glimmered into view: he remembered there was a club near Tottenham Court Road, one that he and Luc had discussed visiting. He could take a bus, go to the club, have a few drinks and sit in a corner until it closed – after all, what other option had he to see out the night? And besides, he always felt safe in clubs.

He sat down on one of the plastic seats of the shelter and huddled inside his coat and tried to will his body to stop its quaking. The bus was a long time in coming and he dozed off momentarily, coming to with a start. He turned to say something to Luc beside him, and found himself staring into the pale face of the girl who had told him the time. She stared back in alarm, then turned away to talk with her boyfriend. A couple of minutes later the bus arrived.

Next thing he knew he was standing by himself on a damp pavement with the empty bus rattling away from him. He was in a wide avenue of a nondescript residential district and there was no one in sight. He remained there for a second, stunned, then, feeling the drizzle at his collar, sought cover in the bus shelter where a window of transport information revealed that he was in Edgware, far away to the north of London. He was glad not to have his watch. He didn't want to know the time.

So great are the distances in the city of London between one familiar point and the next that it would have been unthinkable to attempt to walk back, as he had done in Paris on those many, many nights when the rhythms of the last bus or métro lulled him into stupor and he woke an hour later at some unknown and sinister terminus. How many times he had emerged from the underground into a far flung suburb with the last late cafés closing before him and the gates of the station closing behind him. How many times he had been roughly woken by some tired and irritable bus driver – 'This is where you get off.' When he thought of his life abroad it was often nights such as this that he remembered, and more precisely such moments of the awful lucidity of a drunken awakening, as he stood drowning on the peripheries of a great city, staring at the anonymous boulevards, looming tenements: disfavoured corners of urban misery.

On one notable occasion – in so far as anything was more or less notable in the reaches of Daniel's memory, where the events of his life floated into view as unmoored of context as happenings in dreams – he had resisted the urgings of friends to stay the night and had taken the last train out of Saint-Germain-en-Laye, an elegant village twelve kilometres to the west of Paris, waking dry-mouthed in Boissy Saint-Leger, rather less elegant and fifteen kilometres to the east. Outside the station he fell into conversation with two youths from the same train, a tall blond with shoulder-length hair, called Patrick, and a short, stocky Italian called Enzo. They were on their way to a party on a nearby housing estate, they explained, and would walk him as far as the main arterial road leading to the city. They seemed friendly enough, but even through his wine fuddle Daniel thought he perceived certain covert exchanges of glance, certain collusive little smiles which were not quite pleasant. For safety's sake he gave them a false name, adding that he was American and staying only briefly in France. These days he often told people he was American. As they walked, three abreast, Daniel in the middle, along the grassy edge of the lonely road, grim apartment blocks along each skyline, they complimented him on his French and then began talking of the ever-rising crime statistics in Boissy Saint-Leger. 'People are always getting murdered around here,' they said, 'on this estate. You're lucky to have us with you, on a Saturday night as well.'

They heard a car approaching. Swiftly, as at a pre-arranged signal, his two companions dragged him from the edge and into a deep ditch that ran alongside the road. 'Don't make a noise, don't move.' They watched the car crawl past. 'But it's the police,' protested Daniel. 'All the more reason,' said Patrick. 'Sometimes the police round here are worse than the murderers.'

When the car was out of sight they regained the road. 'So you're not coming to our party then?' said Enzo. 'No, no, I want to get home,' said Daniel. The two youths waved goodbye and set out across the desolate grassland towards the great apartment blocks, and Daniel continued along the road as fast as he could manage.

He had been walking perhaps five minutes when there came a whooping noise near at hand, and the two youths leapt out of the ditch to stand before him. Patrick was wearing a hideous horror-comic smile. 'You see, I'm the murderer,' he said, and Enzo chimed in happily: 'He's completely crazy, you know.' They searched him and found his residency permit which gave away the lie as to his name, nationality, situation in France, and they shook their heads over it as in deep sadness at Daniel's futile stratagem. Panicking completely Daniel apologised for having no money, offered them his watch, his ring. They helped themselves from his cigarettes and then began laughing. 'We were only fooling around, we just wanted to frighten you a little. We're friends all the same, aren't we?' Still uncertain, Daniel managed a laugh of his own, and offered them the rest of the cigarettes as if their joke deserved some reward. They asked for his telephone number and he wrote it on the cigarette packet, no longer daring to falsify the information, as if they were the all-seeing eye of Justice. This time they let him go.

About a kilometre along the road he managed to hitch a lift from a young man in a flashy new car, who agreed to drop him at Bastille. They exchanged few words, and when Daniel bent his head and began to cry softly his driver simply turned up the music on the car radio. It was getting light as they drove along the quays of the Seine; from Bastille Daniel walked to the apartment he was currently occupying near République. He slept for most of the day. When he woke, only the mud from the ditch on his coat and the blisters on his feet could convince him that it was not a dream. Three days later, to his great surprise, Patrick called him, tentative on the other end of the line. Daniel made a vague promise to keep in touch, repeating the boy's telephone number with deliberation as if he were writing it down, knowing all the while that he would never call nor see the pair of them again and already oddly regretting the fact.

Such was the episode that swam back, with hallucinatory clarity into his mind, while he waited for the rain to stop over Edgware, seeming somehow representative of all those nights when he had handed over his fate to dubious strangers in his reckless and drunken loneliness. And the chilling wonder was that – stranded in deserted termini or stumbling through murky sidestreets – he had never been accosted, never been robbed or beaten or murdered, by one drunker or lonelier than himself. He didn't deserve to have been spared so often and so completely. What twisted guardian angel had ensured his safety all those nights? He knew he should be thankful that he was still alive. But he wasn't thankful.

8

Who Likes Children?

Throughout the years of his growing up, until he no longer went there, Daniel could never return to his parents' house without the fear that in his absence somebody had found out something bad about him. Doubtless this anxiety dated back to the period when as a child he stole, when his mother took to regularly searching his room, harvesting the evidence with which to confront him on his return. Later there had been other things for her to find, letters she could open, diaries she could read, all his negligently concealed private life. At thirteen it was a pornographic magazine someone had given him; at sixteen, a half-bottle of vodka he had emptied with a schoolfriend one wild afternoon of the holidays and inexpertly hidden in the depths of his wardrobe; at sixteen again, a scrunched-up cigarette packet. Other items, other ages: a rosary from his shortlived religious phase, an awkward letter from the bank, a dubious book. All these totems of infamy she rooted out during his absences from the house. Nor need the discovery be anything so tangible: someone might telephone him while he was away, and he would be found out in a lie or a truancy. Sometimes she tackled him directly, other times she would wait, sitting absolutely still as the daylight ebbed from the room, her body growing heavy with shadow, face puckered, eyes narrowed, smoking and stubbing out cigarette on cigarette so that the very air around her hung thick with poison. There was no sound in the house, no radio, nothing. She would respond to his greeting with a tight little choke in the throat that could have meant absolutely anything. And for as long as he could endure it he would tiptoe about the house, knowing that soon it would be necessary to go and face her and plead to know what terrible thing he had done this time.

And it was never to leave him, this fear of his own absence, this apprehension of the dangers of being elsewhere. Just the knowledge that two friends of his had met without him was enough to set off the old panic, and though he escaped his parents' home he was never again to share a house, not for a single night, without disquiet accompanying each going out and guilt each return. To travel successfully, to go one's way in the world, requires an assumption Daniel could never make: that people might continue to wish him well while he was not there. And since the dilemma resolved itself into a choice between never being absent or else prolonging his absence indefinitely, between never going out and never coming home again, his whole life became a series of flights, and a series of efforts, never wholly successful, to destroy the evidence and cover the traces behind him.

He got back to Brixton shortly before eight. The trees were very bare along the avenue and up against the windows of the house. In the passageway he failed to locate the light switch and stumbled over somebody's bicycle and cried out in real pain, then swore under his breath at the noise. The house was amazingly shabby in this early light, but to his eyes comfortably so, benign with the concerted neglect of the very different personalities who lived there.

Gently he pushed open the living-room door. Instead of Luc he found Matthew and Fran sitting on the couch, in dressing-gowns, and Saul, a sweater pulled over his pyjamas, at the big table. Matthew was leaning forward, his elbows resting on his knees and his large hands wrapped round a mug of coffee. There were mugs on the table also, and plates with toast crumbs, and a jam-jar and a jar of Marmite. Just as he, climbing the stairs, had listened for their voices, so they had been listening for his footsteps.

Now they watched him as he crossed the room, pulled out a chair, and sat down at the table.

Finally he gave a short laugh. 'I thought you'd all be in bed still.'

There was a moment's silence, then Fran, with an exaggerated sigh, stood up and stretched her undernourished and childlike body. 'Well, if you'll excuse me, I think that's where I'm going. I feel like hell.' She shuffled her way past him to the door, without looking up. 'Bye, Daniel,' she said over her shoulder. 'Bye, boys.'

'See you later, Fran.'

'Bye now, Fran.'

Daniel waited as Matthew laid down his mug on the floor, rubbed his eyes, picked it up again. 'Your friend Luc turned up here at half past six, to collect his things. Fran had to go down to let him in. He was . . . quite frisky.'

'Ah,' said Daniel. 'I'm sorry. Is he—?'

'He's gone, he went straight away. Grabbed his stuff and went. He said to tell you he'll see you back home. He was very apologetic, once he'd calmed down. He brought us a bottle of champagne. As a peace-offering, he said.'

It was then that Daniel noticed a bottle of Piper Heidsieck on the desk, a pink festive ribbon tied around its neck. 'I really am terribly sorry,' he said. 'He does these things sometimes, he's a bit of a – a character.' In spite of himself he smiled. 'I wonder where he got champagne at this time on a Sunday morning.'

Saul put a match to his cigarette and commented with heavy irony: 'Yes. A real "live wire".'

Daniel's smile vanished. 'I'm sorry,' he said.

'It's hardly your fault. True enough,' Matthew conceded, 'I'd sooner not have had the wake-up and not had the champagne either. But I don't suppose he *planned* it. Whatever happened to you, by the way?'

'Last night? Oh – ' He achingly needed to be offered some coffee, and had an aching certainty that he would not be. 'Oh – we split up. I mean, we lost each other. Outside a club.

111

Near Charing Cross. I waited there for him for at least an hour,' he added unnecessarily, unconvincingly.

Still with that severe irony Saul asked: 'And did he have his little friend in tow by that stage?'

Daniel turned his head. 'Friend?'

Matthew said: 'He had somebody with him. Apparently they met in a disco. His name was Jason. They left together. Luc wanted to show him the hotel and the town, he said. They seemed to find this idea hilarious. You may get to meet him. He looked about fifteen years old.'

'Ah,' said Daniel. He glanced down at his hands, then up at Matthew, then at his hands once more. So here was the reason for the early morning council that had awaited him, this the explanation of their accusatory stares and of Fran's abrupt withdrawal. His friends were liberal and tolerant people; swift to defend, cautious to condemn; confronted with something that passed their experience they readily accepted it as proof of their own limitations. Acting on such principles they had extended to Luc, in extending their hospitality, the benefit of the doubt. For his sake – Daniel's sake. And now it was impossible for them not to feel abused in their trust, impossible for them not to see in their old friend Daniel an accessory to the debauch of a child.

He realised all this, of course. He knew these people well and knew the workings of their minds, knew that he would probably, but for France, have turned out much the same and subscribed to the same standards. But beneath the embarrassment, the obvious awkwardness of the situation, what Daniel felt most strongly and immediately was envy. Not a particularised envy of Luc for finding the boy nor of the boy for snaring Luc, nor yet envy for the sweets of sexual exploration the two of them were perhaps enjoying even now. Rather, it was the old and unspecifically erotic throb of envy that Luc never failed to arouse in him, which had first and so fatalistically drawn him into Luc's wake, and made breaking free of him so unthinkable a proposition. It was the knowledge that what Luc dared sober he dared only drunk, experiencing drunk what Luc enjoyed sober. It was the knowledge that Luc, lolling defiantly naked on a beach, or rowdily scandalous in a starched-linen restaurant, was a complete person as he would never be, a vain, infuriating, utterly unreliable totality. It was the knowledge that while he, Daniel, clowned and affected droll voices to win over the playground bullies, in another corner, backed against the fence and furious, Luc put up his little fists and refused to surrender. It was the knowledge, as he pictured the two boys now doubtless frolicking in sleepless hilarity on some empty early Sunday train, that he would never match Luc, because all their attraction for each other rested in the disparity between them.

And as he experienced this lurch of adoring envy, wishing he had been there to appreciate Luc's latest stunt this morning, he consigned his friendship with Matthew, with Fran, with Saul, to the past. He could perhaps have found words sufficiently remorseful, expressions sufficiently placatory to reassure them that he was not irredeemably lost, that he condoned Luc's behaviour no more than they. But he was paralysed by his weird fierce loyalty to Luc, and by the same mesmerised incapacity in the face of disaster which, three years before, had kept him high up in that first tawdry Parisian hotel as the opening of the university year approached, sounded, and passed.

Meanwhile, having made his point, Matthew could afford to be magnanimous. 'You don't really want to go now, surely? If you need a few hours' sleep, well, the bed's still made up.'

'No thanks,' said Daniel, 'I think I'd better be on my way.'

Saul was yawning and stretching. Matthew said: 'Well, let us know if you get down to London again.' Not: come down to London again.

'Thanks.' Daniel stood up, hesitated, made a gesture which took in the pristine camp bed, the bottle of champagne, the cups of stewed coffee on the table. 'Look, we're really sorry about this, you know.' His voice came out at once half-hearted and irritable.

113

'Don't mention it,' said Matthew. It was not an amnesty: it was, precisely, an instruction. 'You can let yourself out, can't you.'

He had to shiver for some fifteen minutes waiting for a bus to take him down Brixton Hill, and then again in the lonely underground. Now the tiredness hit him and he slumped on a bench next to an elderly distinguished-looking black who regarded him strangely. He guessed he must have that unmistakable look of smashed nocturnal revelry about him that he had learned himself to identify as unerringly on the dinner-jacketed ball-hoppers of Cambridge as on the fuzzy stares of the teenage *banlieusards* who descended on Paris each Friday and Saturday, and whose big night out could only end with the first suburban train next morning. There was a kind of momentary freemasonry established between those weekend survivors, as they stood, yawning and blinking, in their fantastic and rumpled party-gear, on station platforms, or huddled in hectic caffeine-intoxication around the tables of dreary cafés. Daniel grinned up at the man next to him and for a second, so full was he of Luc-adoration, considered some Luc-inspired devilment, some provocation. But he was too tired, his mind too sluggish. He fell asleep instantly on the train from Paddington, and almost missed his stop.

Then it was up the hill from the station into the empty centre of town. It was Sunday morning, and cold. The wind seemed almost personal, almost vindictive as it blew through his body, that body which must surely be made up of some substance far less buoyant, less durable, than flesh, so did it shrink and shrivel under the invisible penetrations of this cold. As if sensing his body's vulnerability, the headache he had been holding at bay now pressed itself mutinously into being. Struggling up the hill, Daniel had the impression that he was expending enormous effort for no progress; he felt sick of his body.

In the dull November morning the housefront looked more than ever like a lunatic's vacant face. There was no one about in the downstairs rooms, and Robert's car was missing from the driveway. Daniel wandered through to the kitchen, where the weightier Sunday papers lay untouched alongside the remains of a hurried breakfast. Someone, Megan at a guess, had upended a plastic beaker and the mess had been just left there, a pool of milk forming along the edge of the counter whence it dripped down onto the floor. He looked at the crumbs, the milk, the smears of jam, and the thought of breakfast, of eating something, of turning something over in his mouth, was too much for him. He set the coffee machine to work, selected one of the supplements from the newspaper pile, and began flicking through it, entirely oblivious to any thought but that half an hour later he would be in bed and drifting off to sleep, when all of a sudden the slight, scarcely perceptible alteration in the atmosphere of the house, the minute observed divergences from habit – spilt milk unattended to, the untouched papers, the car gone on a Sunday morning – coalesced into a certainty that something was very wrong. He slammed down the newspaper and pushed it from him as if reading it were an act of sacrilegious frivolity. 'Rachel?' he called out, the forced normality of his voice cracking on the second syllable. He lowered himself from the stool and moved over to the door, calling to his sister again.

There was a clattering of young feet in the hall, and Karl erupted into the room, arms already stretched out for an embrace. Just behind him, kicking out her fat stockinged legs with wobbly determination, came Megan. They were delighted to see him, but with the enervated, slightly whiney joy of recent deprivation or disappointment. Something was wrong, and they didn't understand it and were bored and bothered by it, and they hoped that Daniel's return spelt an end to it, or at the very least promised a distraction.

Rachel stood in the kitchen doorway, her face white and tense. 'I was upstairs,' she explained, 'I had to change Megan.' She leaned against the door-jamb, framed there.

'What's wrong?' Daniel asked.

She looked at him, and just momentarily the tears

threatened to overcome the muscles of her face and throat. 'It's Guy,' she said.

'Is he . . .?' The telephone began ringing. Before she could stop him Karl had slipped past his mother and was cantering through to answer it. She breathed something – 'Oh no, please,' some such thing, Daniel didn't catch it – as she turned after him.

For a few fond seconds he imagined nothing worse than a relapse on Guy's part, a new theft in reaction to the looming bugbear of Belgium, nothing that need concern him, Daniel, since the whole business predated him, was ancient history. And he found himself, for reasons quite selfish, hoping this was in fact the case. And then he realised the vanity of such a hope, and understood what subtle change it was that had been wrought on the atmosphere of his sister's house. Children inhabit a home far more tangibly than adults, inhabit it with their noise, their mess; concepts of conformity and of anonymity are anathema to them: their very existence consists in making their presence felt, and in setting at a spin the immediate world to revolve around them, such that the intimate of a household, only a moment over the threshold, will usually know on his unconscious register how many children are at home and how many away, how many sleeping or awake. And what the house told, what Rachel's face told and the overexcitation of the infants, was the fact that Guy was missing.

Daniel began to feel nauseous. Looking down at his wrist he saw the band of paler skin, and, more than ever convinced that it must have been Guy who took the watch, felt it as a visible brand that implicated him in the boy's new predicament. Then, from a forgotten corner of his mind, came a sudden vivid picture of Luc, that first night, turning at the top of the stairs, with an inquiring nod towards Guy's door. 'That's Guy's room,' Daniel had said, and Luc had smiled with satisfaction. He must see Luc. He should go and settle with Luc.

His niece was pulling at a pile of laundry. With a decisive movement he swept her up in his arms and carried her, kicking deliriously, through to the living room, where Rachel stood talking into the phone. He set Megan down and put his arm round Karl's shoulders to quieten him, and caught what he could of the conversation.

'I told you I'd call you as soon as there was any news. I'm waiting for Robert to come back, he's out with the car . . . No, no . . . well, *I* can't go, can I? . . . Yes, he is, he got back a few minutes ago. I haven't even had a chance to explain.' She half-turned and glanced across at Daniel, to acknowledge his presence as she spoke about him. 'Do you want to talk to him?'

The other person evidently did not wish to talk to Daniel. After hasty goodbyes, assurances, placatory promises, Rachel put the phone down and turned to face her brother. Karl, who had waited through the call with mounting impatience, now began to tug at Daniel's wrist, pleading all the while: 'You want to play? You want to play with Karl?'

'Guy's disappeared,' she said baldly. 'He didn't come home from school on Friday. He was there, he left at the usual time, but he never came home, and no one's seen him since.'

The children had to be appeased. Rachel gave Megan a newspaper to tear to pieces, and pulled down a fresh colouring book for Karl, one she had been saving for Christmas. He was reluctant to accept the bribe, and did so only because the book was so obviously new.

'That was Mother just now. Friday evening I cracked, I had to tell her. The police suggested it anyway, just in case Guy made his way up there. She keeps phoning me up to tell me how worried she is. *I'm* feeling guilty for making *her* worried because *my* son's disappeared. She's threatening to come down. I absolutely don't want her here.'

Daniel could think of nothing to say. He sat down.

'Robert's out with the car now. Scouring the town.'

Briefly she held a hand to her eyes. 'When I was upstairs with Megan and heard the door just now I thought for a second it might be *him*.'

'I'm sorry,' was all he could manage.

'Mummy, this crayon's *broken*.'

'Karl, please, I'm talking to Daniel.' Momentarily she lost her train of thought. Then: 'Anyway, don't *apologise*. It's not your fault, how were you to know?' She glanced at him for a moment before continuing: 'If I'd had a number for you in London I'd have called you. Not that there was anything you could have done.' Suddenly she covered her eyes.

'I'm sorry.'

'Will you *please* not keep on being sorry,' she said with sudden violence. The children were visibly upset. Karl dropped his colouring book and pushed in close: 'Mummy,' he whined, 'Mummy, where's Guy?' She was near to losing control, checked herself just in time and, transforming her very gesture of exasperation, began fretfully to stroke Karl's shiny hair. Then she was ashamed of herself, and Daniel had to look away.

'They don't understand,' she told him wearily. 'I think they thought he was coming back with you.'

'So,' Daniel said, 'how did it happen?'

She waited a moment, ostensibly for Karl's attention to wander back to his sister, busy dismembering a newspaper on the other side of the room. He ambled off to torment her. Rachel said: 'I don't think he's run away. The police don't seem to think so either. He took nothing with him. He went to school on Friday, absolutely as normal, the whole day. When he didn't come home I called Jamie Wilke's house. Guy had told Jamie he wasn't going straight home, he was going to walk through the town. Robert went out in the car, looking for him. When he got back we decided to call the police.'

'And?'

'It was quite unpleasant. They wanted to know if we'd been having any problems with him. Of course, they assumed he was Robert's son, and when it came out that he wasn't, they asked all sorts of questions about Guy's father, as if *he* could have had something to do with it.'

'Is it so impossible?'

She didn't bother replying. 'Then they said to contact

118

Mother and the rest of the family, in case he showed up there. They must have gone to talk to Jamie Wilke, too, because yesterday Jamie's mother called round. She'd brought me a cake – can you imagine? I suppose she was trying to be kind. But she also told me something about Guy. You remember how he was late home from school on Tuesday, and he said he'd been to the park with Jamie. Well, that wasn't true. Jamie was off school, and we don't know where Guy went on Tuesday. It would make it easier . . .' She broke off.

'Yes?'

'It would make it easier if Guy told the truth.'

They sat side by side on the sofa. This is my sister, Daniel told himself, we're supposed to be so close. Down in London wasn't I priding myself on our having grown so close? He knew he should be hugging her, comforting her, drawing her tears. He was quite incapable. He asked: 'What happens now?'

She shook her head. 'We thought maybe there'd been an accident, but the local hospitals have all been checked. They put out an announcement this morning on the local radio station, to be repeated every hour, you know, a description of Guy, the times and so on. I don't hold out much hope of his appearing up north. If for some reason he took it into his head to go and say hello to Mother he'd have got there long since.'

'What about the newspapers?'

'Well, we missed the local paper, and it's too early for the nationals. And it's Sunday. No, there's nothing much we can do except wait.' There was an interruption: Megan began to protest loudly because Karl had snatched some particularly important morsel of newspaper. Rachel intervened and retrieved it for her, then resumed her seat. 'We wait. The police are doing what they can, I suppose. Which is asking around and keeping their eyes open and . . .' Once again she broke off.

'And what?'

'And keeping an eye on various people they know of who . . . who like children.'

Suddenly Daniel was on his feet. 'I have to go out,' he said. 'I'm sorry, I have to go out, I won't be long.' But he didn't at once move, he stood there, swaying, as if slightly drunk.

'Daniel!' She was indignant. 'Where are you going? What is this?'

'I'm sorry, Rachel,' he said, making a grab for his coat, not looking at her. 'I'm sorry. I have to go out. Half an hour. I don't feel too well. I need some air.'

She stood up, called out his name again, but he was already at the front door, and then outside in the chill midday. Lunchtime on a Sunday: the hotel was always busy. Oh, well, what did that matter now, what did it matter who saw him, heard him?

Solange was behind the desk. She stood up as he entered the lobby, surprised. 'Daniel! You've missed Robert,' she said. 'He left half an hour ago. Is there any news?'

'You know about this then?'

Solange nodded.

'It's not Robert I came to see. It's Luc. No, there's no news. Guy's still missing. It's Luc I came to see. Is he back yet?'

Solange stared at him. 'Well, I'm sure I don't know. I rather thought the two of you were together. I wasn't expecting either of you till tomorrow.'

He went through to the staff quarters at the back of the hotel. He was full of decision; all he lacked were the necessary words to say to Luc, to confront Luc. He knocked, and Luc's voice, pitched a little higher than usual, called out from inside: 'Who is it?' And just behind it, scarcely audible, there was an intake of breath and something which might have been a giggle.

'It's me, Daniel,' he said, and pushed open the door.

The curtains were drawn and only the tiny bedside lamp was lit. The room was yellow and overheated, all the more so with the outmoded tropical wallpaper swarmingly busy in this artificial light. Clothes were everywhere, spilling out of drawers, issuing from the open wardrobe, smothering the chairs, peering over the rim of the washbasin, strewn across the floor, an orgy of clothes, for surely not one person alone could be responsible for all these clothes. On the bedside table, on the desk, empty glasses collected, a line of empty beer bottles stood against the wall. Cigarette smoke hung on the stagnant air, mingling with the various odours of alcohol, perfume, and sickly talcum powder, and there were pools of spilt powder over the brown carpet.

Luc was halfway across the room, on his way to answer the door. He stood there now, naked, with a toothglass of whisky hanging from his hand. His head was thrown back slightly, there was a broad smile on his face, and he gave off the dull buzz of alcohol, an erotic blur like a nimbus around him. To Daniel in that moment he appeared as the source of all light and strength, absolutely hard and powerful and somehow terrifying, so perfectly made was he and so complete. All the questions Daniel had prepared on his journey here drained from his head.

There was a stirring in the far corner of the room. Hiding in the bed, clutching at the duvet in giggly embarrassment, was a boy. He was half-in, half-out of a pair of old-fashioned prep-school brushed cotton pyjamas, evidently not his own. He squinted out from his pillow at the intruder.

'You'd better close the door,' Luc ordered. He moved towards Daniel, who found himself edging slightly backwards. 'I wasn't expecting you,' said Luc, 'but now you're here why don't you join us? I always knew you'd come round eventually.' The boy on the bed gulped with laughter again, but this time there was real apprehension in it, of a scene or crisis. 'This is Jason, by the way,' Luc explained. 'We met up last night. Well? Aren't you going to introduce yourself?'

He was right up against Daniel now, and his scent – the cologne, the whisky, his skin, his whole aromatic pitiless carnality – was overpowering. Daniel tried to swallow, choked with disappointment and exclusion and anger. And here before him was Luc, master of the orgy, laughing at his

confusion, mocking his distress as if it were no more than
virgin bashfulness. Suddenly Luc seized him by the back of
the neck, bent his head, kissed him heavily on the mouth for
some seconds; then stood back a pace to survey the result,
nodding in his satisfaction. Daniel stared, his mouth hanging open as Luc's mouth had left it. Then he struck him hard
across the face.

The boy gave a gasp and flinched back among the pillows. Luc's nose had begun to bleed, and he spent a
moment crouched on the edge of the bed, applying a paper
tissue. When he was done he came back and took Daniel by
the shoulder. As if shell-shocked, Daniel allowed himself to
be led and seated in the one chair that the room contained.
Luc looked hard down at him and, when he spoke, his voice
was firm: 'The least we can do is offer you a drink. I know
it's maybe a bit early, but to tell you the truth, we haven't
really stopped. And you look like you need it.' He sloshed a
generous amount of whisky into a mug and pressed it into
Daniel's right hand, which was shaking so much that Luc
took his left hand, also, and placed it around the mug.
Daniel lifted the mug to his mouth and managed to drink
something from it. Meanwhile the boy ventured out from
the bed and joined Luc, kneeling behind him and slipping
his arms around Luc's waist. He blinked across at the stunned visitor.

'Don't worry about Jason here,' said Luc. 'No secrets from
him. Suppose you tell us what's happened.'

He was so calm, so reasonable, so inhuman, sitting naked
on his bed with his lascivious child, interrogating Daniel.
Daniel felt a sudden pressure at his own stomach, in just
those places where the boy's fingers tightened on Luc.

'Danny? Is it Guy? Is that the problem? *Danny*?'

The room tilted dramatically, the mug fell to the floor, he
was staring down at the whisky that soaked into the carpet.
He struggled to his feet. 'Outside,' Luc ordered.

Somehow he was up and out in the corridor. He reached
for another door, finally gripped the handle. It was locked,
so he threw up right there, violently. Luc appeared in the

doorway behind him, knotting a dressing gown and saying his name, but Daniel, choked with heaving coughs, was stumbling towards the exit, and fresh air.

9

Manipulating the Phantoms

'Has your little boy been up to anything a bit naughty that you know of?'

This had been the police sergeant, that Friday of Guy's disappearance, while far away in London Daniel and Luc sat on the floor of the Brixton house, drinking wine and discussing the evening to come. Rachel had waited with growing disquiet until seven o'clock before calling the parents of Jamie Wilke, Guy's current best friend. Then she had called round the parents of such other friends of Guy's as she knew. They were polite and regretful – a few expressed genuine concern – she wondered why she felt a measure of reserve in the reaction of each one of them. Why should they disapprove of her? What could they know? They had no idea, these other mothers, of her history, no cause to condemn her for bringing her delinquent lovechild into their midst. I'm growing paranoid, she told herself, replacing the receiver after the fourth such call. She wondered how widespread was Guy's reputation as a thief.

'Is there any reason you can think of as to why he might have run away?'

There would be no one at the school until Monday morning, but one of the mothers was able to supply the home number of Guy's form mistress. The teacher was flustered, she had just that moment arrived home. Yes, Guy had been at school all day, had left at the usual time. No one had noticed anything odd about him.

Rachel decided he must have run away, and searched his

room for confirmation. There was nothing gone, no practical possessions or precious ones. No food gone from the kitchen. Reluctantly she checked her own purse, then the drawer in her bedroom where she kept some cash. None was missing.

'Where would he run to?' said Robert. 'You haven't been fighting. Why should he run away?'

'Kids do things,' she said, with that irritating authority of hers, as if he knew nothing whatever of children, having come to parenthood so much later than she and in circumstances so much easier. 'They do things, you can't ask why. Why should he steal, if it comes to that?' But she was already abandoning her own theory. She stood in the middle of the kitchen and shuddered. 'What if someone's taken him? There was that car that was hanging around here.'

'Darling, that was months ago.'

'I want you to call the police.'

'Was he happy at school, in his home life, Mrs Phillips?'

The children were put to bed but didn't remain quiet long, for two police officers arrived and at once requested a search of the house and garden. 'You'd be astonished in how many cases the child turns out to be hiding somewhere on the property. Think of it, madam: a little boy, a little girl, they've done something a bit naughty, they're scared of being punished. They can be very ingenious when it comes to finding some little place you'd never think of looking. Has your little boy been up to anything a bit naughty that you know of?'

Rachel forced herself to attend to him: he was asking her a question. She was acutely conscious of her disorderly household, the piles of washing, the toys underfoot. Hardly the home of well-kept children. 'No, of course not,' she said hurriedly.

The policeman smiled, nodded, said again: 'You'd be surprised.' Where law and childhood intersect, there are secrets even she could not guess at, apparently. 'You say the shed is always locked, madam. Well, could you get me a key?'

They requested a picture of Guy. As Rachel went through an old album the senior police officer remarked: 'I couldn't help noticing as we were looking through the house. There's someone else staying here with you?'

'Yes, my brother. He's living with us for a while. He's waiting to move down to London.'

'And where is your brother at the moment?'

'In London. He went down for the weekend, to visit some friends.'

'When did he leave?'

'This afternoon. About three.'

'So he knows nothing about all this.'

'No. Nothing.' She handed over the photograph. 'It's not the most recent, but I think it gives you a fair idea of him.' She watched as he slipped the picture between two sheets of paper.

'Nice-looking little boy. Thank you,' he said. 'Now, if you don't mind, could we just go through this form?'

'Yes, of course, but can I just go upstairs and settle the children?'

The policeman turned to Robert. 'Then perhaps the boy's father . . .?' There was a silence. Rachel and Robert did not look at each other. 'Is there some problem?'

Robert said smoothly: 'None at all. Except that I should apologise for not making things clear sooner. I am Guy's stepfather.'

'Oh — ?' said the policeman. He glanced at Robert once more. 'Well, Mrs Phillips, I'm sure I can wait until you've seen to your children.'

Robert poured some tea for the policemen, who treated him now with the deferential politeness reserved for a potential suspect. 'Don't let yourselves panic, Mr Phillips. Nine times out of ten there's a very simple explanation. Most kids get up to these kind of pranks at one time or another. I don't suppose he was in the habit of it, your – the little boy?'

'No.'

'Never ran away, nothing like that?'

'Nothing more than fits of temper. He'd storm off and be back within half an hour.'

'Oh — ?' said the policeman. 'They were frequent occurrences, these fits of temper?'

'About as frequent as with any kid his age, I suppose.'

'And how frequent is that?'

Robert said: 'I'm sorry?'

'You said it happened as frequently as with any child his age. How frequently is that?'

'Really I – ' He stopped, laughed briefly.

'Do you have children of your own, Mr Phillips?'

Robert paused, laid down his cup, and said quietly: 'The children upstairs are mine.'

Rachel rejoined them, and together they filled out the routine bureaucracy of the disappearance. 'Now,' said the policeman, 'is there any reason you can think of as to why he might have run away? Had there been any trouble? A quarrel, perhaps?'

'None,' said Rachel. 'Apart from the usual things.'

'And what are the usual things, please?'

Robert suppressed a gesture of irritation. Rachel said wearily: 'Oh, stupid things, little things. Like not going to bed on time, not tidying his room. Not getting his own way. Normal things.'

The policeman looked up at Robert for confirmation. 'Mr Phillips?' Apparently they were not to be treated as a couple. 'Was he happy at school? No history of bullying, truancy?'

'Not that I'm aware of,' said Rachel. 'And we would know.'

'Now,' said the policeman. 'I'm going to have to ask you for some names, addresses, phone numbers. His "pals", his teachers if you know them, any family he has living locally – in fact, anyone around here who might know him.'

'We must have tried them all already,' said Rachel, but she gave the information he requested. 'We have no family locally,' she then said.

'And what family do you have elsewhere?'

127

'Apart from my brother, who's here with us, there are my parents up in Leeds. There are his great-aunts, too – my mother's sisters and their families. They are all up in Leeds, too, or nearby. And, oh – there are cousins of mine, abroad, in Canada . . .'

'Your son is close to your parents?'

'Well, yes. Obviously they don't see as much of each other as they might like – the distance and so on. But yes, they're close enough.'

'And your parents would contact you if the boy were suddenly to turn up there? Even if he asked them not to?'

'It's extremely unlikely that he'd do such a thing,' said Rachel. 'But yes: my mother would certainly ring me straightaway.' And so she would, reflected Rachel: *What have you done to the poor little boy now?*

'Have you spoken to your mother yet about this?'

'No. I was going to call her when you'd finished.'

'Thank you,' said the policeman. Then, addressing them both: 'And what about family on the father's side?'

Robert smiled and said drily: 'They all live in Switzerland. I was born in Lausanne and my parents still live out there. I don't think even an extreme fit of temper would prompt Guy to chase off to Lausanne.'

'Quite,' said the policeman, looking up at him. 'And thank you for telling me, sir. But I was referring to the child's real father.'

Robert's face darkened. 'Ah yes,' he said. 'I'm sorry.'

The senior policeman smiled, sipping his superior knowledge, and his colleague made a note.

Daniel returned from the hotel sickly and furtive. In the living room Robert was standing, still in his great overcoat, by the window. Walking through the door Daniel caught and understood the expression that passed for a pleading second across Rachel's face, the hope and the crushing disappointment, just such a look as must have passed a few moments ago, when Robert returned. And he had a sudden intuition of how it would be, each time she heard the door, as the days passed and the years, if Guy was not found.

Found. He cursed himself even for thinking it, anything sooner than that. Guy was lying in a ditch somewhere perhaps, injured, shivering with cold, bound and gagged if need be, but still alive. *Found.* The thought was a betrayal in itself, as if a moment's pessimism might loosen the boy's life-thread.

Robert stood there in his big coat as Karl danced around him. 'Guy was in the tea shop in Dean Street Friday afternoon. He went in there about four o'clock. He sat down for about ten minutes but he didn't order anything. He looked as if he was waiting for someone. Then he got up and left.'

'Do they know where?' asked Rachel.

'No idea.'

She took hold of Karl's hand and pulled him towards her, as if he too required protection from the cruel facts of the cruel world. 'Is that all?'

'No.' Robert was pulling at his coat. 'No. He'd been there before, that's why they noticed him. He was in there on Tuesday, with a man, middle-aged, distinguished-looking they said, glasses. Spoke with an accent. They think he could have been a foreigner.'

Rachel released Karl and reached for her cigarettes. 'They're sure it was Guy?'

'Absolutely. I spoke to the girl who served them, it was the same girl in on Friday. I showed her the picture. She couldn't say much about the man, what he was wearing and so on. They had two cakes each. The man didn't touch his, apparently. In the end Guy ate them. And they had something to drink, the girl thinks it was hot chocolate.'

Hot chocolate. Guy pleading, cajoling, on a dozen evenings already this winter. 'Oh, Guy – we don't have enough milk,' Rachel might say. 'Maybe tomorrow night you can have some.'

'A foreigner,' Rachel said. Neither of them looked at Daniel. Then she asked: 'How did he seem, did she say? Did he look frightened? Is it possible Guy was acting . . . under duress?'

Robert exploded in his helpless impatience. 'Rachel, a kid of nine doesn't consume four cream cakes and a cup of hot chocolate under *duress*.'

But he may, he may, thought Daniel, sitting there between them. People have taken sweeter things in fear and under duress. Robert was listing the roads he had crawled, the places he had stopped to examine. 'Daniel,' Rachel then said, 'thinks we should look again down by the bridge, he thinks Guy may have gone down there.'

Daniel protested: 'That's not what I said. I only meant that it was one of Guy's favourite places and maybe . . .'

'That's where you and he used to go off together,' she said loudly.

'Why are we all so jumpy?' demanded Robert. 'Why are we all so guilty? It's not getting us anywhere.'

They knew it, of course. They tried to speak calmly. But the guiltiness wouldn't go away, and all afternoon the simplest enquiry sounded accusatory. There was Daniel's guilt: that he was to blame in some as yet undefined way, that he had been down in London when it happened, having what passed for a good time. There was Robert's guilt: that this was not his own child, his care not possibly that of a father. There was Rachel's guilt: that she had not been watchful enough, which was in any case the guilt they all shared, and which a child's disappearance, like a suicide, will inevitably prompt. There was the guilt of thinking about other things when Guy was paramount, then the guilt of neglecting precisely those other concerns. Finally there was guilt at the fears they darkly entertained and guilt at not speaking their fears aloud.

Soon the children, fractious, confused and demanding, provided a welcome diversion. Daniel excused himself: 'I've been sick, I've really got to lie down.'

'Oh, go then,' said Rachel, waving him away.

He went to his room and closed the door. He checked behind the bedside table where his watch might have fallen.

He looked under the bed and in various drawers, shook out the duvet and pillows: Karl might well have found it and hidden it, for a joke. Once satisfied that the watch was gone, he lay down on his bed and pondered its disappearance and the disappearance of his nephew. As the churning in his stomach subsided he dozed off, waking again at the sound of raised voices downstairs in the unhappy house. He caught a few of Rachel's words – 'It was you, with your precious job in Brussels, your nagging on about Brussels . . .' – then buried his head in the pillow until he slept, deeply this time, in his certainty and resignation.

Robert knocked up some dinner soon after six and the children were taken up to bed earlier than usual, Karl complaining lustily all the while. Daniel cleared and Rachel did the dishes. Then they switched on the television news as Rachel settled to some needlework. Further details were emerging from a case of serious and long-term child abuse in a foster home in the Midlands.

Daniel glanced up at his sister, who had become very still in her chair. No one wanted to comment on the report or suggest turning it off, and they endured the tawdry story until a studio newscaster reappeared with the comparatively cheerful news of Britain's continued economic decline.

Robert stood up: 'I'm going to bed.' When he was gone Rachel lowered the volume and turned her unhappy face towards her brother. 'I used to think I worried overmuch. But you read about these things happening and it's all on the television and you can't help imagining it for yourself. A couple of weeks back I was in the village with Karl and Megan, we'd been shopping. We sat on a bench next to this man, he must have been about fifty or so. He was very friendly, very taken with Megan. He kept talking to her and saying what a pretty little girl she was. And I kept my arm so tightly around her . . . And all the time I was thinking, stop it, he just wants to be friendly, he's just a man who likes children. But you can't help imagining. And Karl. I see how friendly he is with strangers. He's got so much confidence,

131

he'll go up and talk to anyone – in the park, in the super-market – I would never have done that at his age. And I don't want him to lose that confidence, I don't want him to be afraid of everybody, the way I was. But how can you know what people really want from your children?'

She went back to her mending while Daniel read a maga-zine, glancing up from time to time at the flickering images of the soundless television, and more occasionally at his sister in her stoic absorption, like Penelope daily weaving, nightly unweaving the fabric of her raiment, unfinishable comforter. Stoicism answers to time, not pain: the time until the telegram bearing news of deliverance or fatality, the time between the separate blows to the prisoner beaten in the darkened chamber. Why, he had asked Rachel long ago, do babies cry out with such anguish? Their hunger, their colic, are not pain any worse than we might feel. And she had tried to explain: no worse, certainly, but so much less familiar. And, awaiting memory and with it any notion of a future, of relief, of forgetfulness, their pain absorbs time as a sponge water. 'Rachel,' he said.

She was staring ahead, quite lost in her own thoughts. At the sound of his voice she lowered her eyes to where his horrified gaze was riveted. Her mending lay unravelled in her lap, and the white fabric was spotted with bloodstains, three or four of them, smaller than a penny, from where she had pricked the fleshy ball of her thumb, not once, but over and over.

She fell to crying weakly, for a moment, then went off to the bathroom to dress her thumb. Daniel sat on, helpless, acutely aware of his own helplessness: he wouldn't even have known where band-aids were kept in this house, where to find antiseptic; he wouldn't even have known how to dress a pinpricked finger. His recent thoughts of his sister's stoicism echoed now, mockingly: hadn't that been merely the salve he had applied to his own conscience?

When she returned her face was bright from washing, an attempt to disguise her crying. She brought out a bottle of wine for him to open, switched off the television and put some Bach concerti on the stereo. They played cards, an endlessly complicated version of canasta with which traditionally the family had whiled away diluvian afternoons in the rented holiday cottage in Scotland. Games in the Marriner family had always been associated with minor catastrophe, with prolonged convalescences, flooded picnics, incarcerated Boxing Days, the silences imposed by their mother's migraines. These games were played in an atmosphere of frayed nerves and flayed sensibilities, with much appeasement and diplomacy and prudent reluctance to win too often or too overwhelmingly.

At one point he paused in the act of dealing out the cards. 'Rachel.'

'What?'

'I went to New York last year, you know.' She laid aside the material, as if settling to hear one of his stories: Danny, in his sweet misguided way, trying to distract her from her boredom as so often during the long afternoons of the summer. But there was no story this time, nothing to tell. He wanted simply to explain the price that she was now paying, explain what contracts he had made in his past and in a foreign country, what those prizes were for which he had mortgaged his own and her present serenity. And from the blur of that glamorous fly-by-night life of his, the dancing years, all he could conjure were the topless towers of Manhattan, all he could manage was: 'I went to New York last year.' It was small amends.

She waited, too tired for irritation. 'And? Did you have a nice time there?'

He laughed once, and gave it up. 'It was hell,' he said.

They heard the same tape over and over. To choose another cassette would be to acknowledge that they had listened to, perhaps even enjoyed the first. After about an hour Rachel conceded defeat and said she didn't feel up to playing any more. Daniel returned to his magazine. When he looked up a few moments later she was asleep.

He crossed the room and lowered the volume of the stereo. Rachel's mouth hung slightly open but her small hands were clenched tight. Her sleep betrayed the toll of these last days: this was what he had done to her. He was responsible. And to compound his guilt he knew that a part of her anxiety worked also for him, her sleep beat also with concern for him, in her innocent distress that he had not been spared their trouble. It was evident in the pains she took not to show him the extent of her despair, in the way she bit back her natural vexation if he was nearby, in the way she lashed out at her own husband sooner than at him, the brother who had caused it all.

Tessa the collie was already curled up beside her. Some time later Lily, the mongrel bitch, wandered into the room and settled behind the armchair. Finally it was Lawrence, most arrogant of cats, who, tentative now, came to this room where the lights still burned and the music played on, almost inaudibly, and stayed to sleep. Like the others, Lawrence had been rescued from an RSPCA pound of animals marked for destruction. Upstairs Robert lay across the bed, pole-axed with delayed exhaustion, and Karl slept and Megan slept, their childish knowledge that something was wrong subdued to the imperatives of growing, feeding, learning, retaining, and the imperative of forgetting what was irrelevant or a hindrance to this.

Waifs and strays. As a child of eight she had secreted a starving kitten into the cat-loathing home of her parents, since when it was a family joke that Rachel could not see an abandoned animal without wanting to adopt it. His sister's concern over Daniel's rootless idleness, her worries over the nocturnal flights of Lawrence, in fact the most brazen and bellicose fighter in the village, her disproportionate regret if ever she caught herself showing impatience or ill-temper and her swift mortification when she struck out physically or verbally at her children – all these were of a piece with the excessive delicacy prompted by scenes of televised sex or violence, the discomfort if ever Daniel recalled to her the particularly bitchy wit of his university or Paris contemporaries, the inability to harbour grudges or even criticise for any length of time, the physical flinching from the mere thought of cruelty to any animal or human being, at whatever remove. There was nothing the least saintly in her attitude, nothing admirable even: it was a purely nervous aspect of her constitution, as little responsive to her will as an allergy.

He woke her at two and watched her climb, swaying with fatigue, the stairs to bed. The house was quiet at last. How many nights had they waited for this quiet, greeted it with relief, the quiet which meant that Karl and Megan were finally sleeping and dreaming about the unconscious work of children. But tonight it was different; the quiet of the house was also Guy's absence from it, and if the adults slept at all it was only an imperfect vigilance, and in despite of the telephone which intruded with its stillness on their rest.

It was after three when Daniel went to his room. He turned on the light and looked around. He had moved so many times in his life and at such short notice that he was skilled in sorting out the essential from the ephemeral, at packing his twenty-three years into, as it might be, one suitcase and one shoulder bag. He acquired nothing without unconsciously deciding whether it would outlast the next migration, so that some shirts were sparingly preserved while others were outworn quickly and then abandoned, some letters kept while others were forgotten in a drawer, or else torn across and dumped in the wastepaper basket with no more ceremony than a litter of bills and circulars. He was almost proud of this ruthlessness: that at any moment he could compress his life into ninety by sixty by thirty centimetres, leaving nothing behind that might adhere to him and trace him.

This time it was more difficult. He had to go quickly and noiselessly. Always he had been astonished at the carelessness with which people left lying around little bits of their past for others to find: now there was no help for it, he was obliged to do likewise. He took what clothes he could, but the lighter ones, the summer ones: he would buy sweaters at the other end. Then he sorted the letters he had received since his return to England.

135

Most of them he could safely leave; they were dull replies to dull letters he had written himself in the early boredom and loneliness, from people he would never contact again. He thought, with a familiar regret disciplined by the years, of Matthew, of Fran, of Saul, whom he would never contact again. He had their address; behind it was a house he had known, slept in. He would never use that address now.

Then there were older letters, from the days when he had written intensely and at length. The many letters from Fran's mother, that remarkable woman; from his own parents in his first year at Cambridge; from Jennie who had loved him, Saul who had loved him, Fran whom he had loved. University letters: the birthday greetings, exam good luck wishes, the dutiful postcards they had exchanged in that heady first summer vacation of sworn undying comradeship, that year before Daniel went off to France and didn't come back. He looked through them. If he kept one it would be the same as keeping them all.

He pushed the dead letters into their chocolate box and replaced them on the topmost bookshelf. Then he turned to the photographs, a mere handful. Two of them were stuck together with what looked like dried coffee; some had their corners bent back; others curled from hanging on various walls. He ought to start an album, he told himself. He put the photos into their envelope and zipped it into a side pocket of his bag. He would never keep an album. How would he ever find a place for it in his luggage?

That was the hard part done. He packed a couple of books, thinking of the journey ahead, and a few cassettes. He snapped one more into the Walkman and left its box lying open on the desk.

At some point Megan woke up and cried a little, and Daniel stood very still in the middle of the room, scarcely breathing. If Megan roused them they would see the light under his door. And yet what of it? He was often awake at this hour, and his sister was far too respectful to come and disturb him. In the event Megan cried softly for a moment and then there was silence once more.

His hands shook. In Paris it had been quite commonplace that he would wake with this trembling of his hands, which would never altogether stop throughout the day. He wrote it off as no more than alcoholic shakes, had thought his hands would cease to tremble with time, within the relative temperance of his sister's household. Now he thought they would never cease, not while the least stubborn remnant of the past quivered for life within him, not while the faintest ghost of a childhood fear stirred him into wakefulness in the teeming four o'clock night, not while his parents retained the power, in any darkened bedroom of his mind, to say: no, it is only a rucked curtain, or else: yes, you are right, there *is* an imp crouching there in the window. Not while the grown-ups continued to manipulate the phantoms.

When he was done he set the alarm clock for six-thirty, knowing how little good these few snatched hours of sleep would do, knowing he would do better to see out the night. But he was sagging on his feet. He crossed to the window and reached out for the curtains.

Looking down at the square of garden, the path, the pavement under its streetlamp, he had an image of himself as he would be in a few hours' time, in the grey morning, stealing from the house, turning to look back at its windows, then hitching the bag firmly onto his shoulder and setting off down the road, ungainly with his burden, almost running. He saw himself with recognition and regret, the one at the window, the one in the street; it was like saying goodbye. But he wondered which was the real one, which he would be left with. He lay down on the bed in his clothes and switched off the light.

Before sleep could take him he prayed. The activity was so long unfamiliar to him that he said the words out loud, not trusting his mind to concentrate in the silence. He prayed that he was about to do the right thing, rather as he might have prayed that a coin tossed into the air should land propitiously for him. He prayed for Rachel and all her kindnesses, and for the hurt he was going to do her and for its swift healing, and he prayed for her young children, Megan and Karl, dreaming their way into life, and for the other children yet to live. Most of all he prayed for Guy: 'Let him come back soon and safely, and without memories. And until then, please God, don't let them harm him. Because they might harm him.'

———— 10 ————

The World Without Him

When Robert awoke and saw his wife, tense in her sleep, beside him, he called his office and told them not to expect him. Then he brought her a mug of tea. She twisted in the bed, pushed at the upheaval of covers, spoke to him without opening her eyes. 'I feel terrible,' she said. 'What time is it?'

'I'm taking the day off work,' he said. 'You sleep on if you want to.' He laid a hand on her forehead and then brushed away her hair. She groaned, twisted away from him, buried her face in the pillow.

The children were already stirring as normal. He took them downstairs and gave them breakfast. Karl was particularly rowdy and wouldn't leave Megan alone, so Robert took them out in the car, first to the shops, for there were things to buy and they had been neglectful of the shopping, and then to the station to watch the trains.

Rachel was woken about an hour later by the telephone.

She sat straight up in bed and felt the cold on her forehead. 'Hello? Hello?'

But it was only her mother. 'Well, what is he *doing*, then?' she enquired after Robert. 'Of course, you can't expect him to feel the same way, it's not his child. Are you sure you wouldn't rather I came down?'

Rachel felt like weeping. To be brought to consciousness for this. 'Quite sure,' she said.

'What about your brother?'

'He's asleep at the moment, I suppose. We were up until

very late. He's being very supportive.' She was already looking around for a cigarette: the first cigarette of the day, its unfamiliar, lurching dizziness, that would shut out her mother's words for a few seconds.

'Hm. Well. I'm glad there's someone who can sleep. What was he up to in London, by the way? I don't like the thought of you down there on your own.'

'I'm not on my own, Mum.' With quiet despair she remembered that her cigarettes were downstairs, amidst the debris of the night.

'As good as. Listen. I'll ring you again this evening. And tomorrow I'm coming down. No buts. How can I leave you down there with the two little 'uns and this thing preying on your mind? You say you're managing—'

'It's very kind of you, but—'

'Why are you always so stubborn? Why do you have to insist everything's under control?'

'Because I really don't think it would help anybody if you came down. Really. Look, Mum, goodbye.' She put down the phone, held it down for a moment as if stifling the clamorous, insistent life from her mother.

The house was eerie without voices. She made herself some coffee. She was quite without appetite. When the phone rang she was afraid it might be her mother again, and briefly, insanely, considered ignoring it. The police: nothing to report. When she returned to the kitchen her cigarette had slipped from the ashtray and burned a mark onto the breakfast bar. She burst into weak tears, for the first time that day, then took a shower and began to feel a little better, collected some washing, was hauling it bravely through to the machine, then had to sit down to cry again.

She forced herself to leave her brother sleeping. She prepared a salad for lunch, taking infinite pains with each morsel, each leaf: they had to eat, after all. When by one o'clock Daniel had still not made an appearance she took him some coffee. Her first thought, when she saw his empty room, was that he must have gone out with Robert and the children. Then she noticed that his bag was missing. Perhaps he was away for the day, down to London again, to escape the atmosphere. Strange that he should have left no message, but the Daniel of old had been thoughtless and impulsive; it was only in these last months that he had signalled his comings and goings with such thoughtful care, laboriously explaining that he was off to the library and would be back in one hour, was off to London and would call to announce his return. His dressing-gown was where he had thrown it over the bed, his books and papers lay in their customary disorder across the desk. She was angry with him for abandoning her, angry that she couldn't blame him for doing so; most of all she was sad to be alone.

Robert came back with the children, whom he had not succeeded in tiring out, and they all sat down to lunch. Karl wouldn't eat; he screamed at the top of his lungs and ended by throwing his plate onto the floor. Rachel lashed out at him and then began crying once more. Briefly the house was chaos. They took Karl up to bed where he screamed hysterically for ten minutes before suddenly fading into sleep with the delayed exhaustion of contagious anxiety. Megan was quite happy to sit in her high chair playing with Robert's bunch of keys; they fascinated her. Rachel and Robert could barely speak; for an hour they loathed each other. Then Megan began crying in her turn and Rachel broke down again and Robert, stricken with remorse, was able to comfort her. She huddled into her armchair, a tissue shredded in her fist.

There were other moments of hysteria, too painful, too normal to dwell upon. In the late afternoon Rachel's mother called. Robert was already reaching across with the phone when Rachel made a sharp negative gesture. He then explained: 'Rachel's lying down just now, I don't want to disturb her.' He hung up and turned apologetically: 'I don't think she believed me. She said you had words this morning.'

'She was pressurising me. She wants to come down.'

It was their own helplessness they saw in each other and hated. All activities seemed impossible and obscenely

141

frivolous. Robert turned on the television and Rachel couldn't bear it. The thought of dinner, of a drink before or instead of dinner, was terrible. Rachel developed a specific fear: which was that she wouldn't be able to hold the pans or plates, that her hands would not control the matches for the gas, the lid of the earthenware casserole, the knives. The fear grew until she was almost incapable of lifting the mugs of black coffee made foully strong, which was all they drank throughout the afternoon. There was some distraction when Karl awoke. He walked around the living room in a daze, rubbing his eyes and brushing away his hair, frowning in perplexity at the uncoordination of his not yet wholly wakened body. They ate sandwiches, sitting around the blank TV screen. Robert played with the children for half an hour, unable to disguise his apathy, then gave up and switched on the television, but Karl insisted on sitting right in front of it, his large head blocking out the screen, refusing to move. So Rachel took them upstairs, bathed them, and put them to bed.

As if all this were not enough she next became edgy about Daniel. It no longer seemed conscionable that he should disappear without a word; it chimed in too well with the prevailing mood of catastrophe. 'I hope nothing's happened to him,' she said, and added, not knowing why: 'He *is* my brother, after all.'

'He's old enough to look after himself,' said Robert, alert to any sign of a renewed Marriner clannishness. 'He's probably gone off to clear his head.'

Rachel stood up. 'Do you know, I'm going to call the hotel. Maybe that friend of his knows something.' But when she asked to speak to Luc Braillon a voice informed her that he was no longer working at the hotel.

Again they sat in silence for a while, but this new Daniel-related anxiety had by now communicated itself to Robert. He said: 'I don't like that boy and I don't trust him. There was something not quite right about the way he just turned up like that. How do we know where he's from?'

142

'He's just a friend of Daniel's, that's all. It was good for Daniel to have him here.'

'Well, I didn't like him.' He sat quiet for a moment and then said: 'I'm going to speak to Solange.' He called the hotel once more. 'Solange, look, this French boy, this Luc . . .' Rachel was amazed to find she had been chewing her nails at intervals throughout the past few hours. She lit a cigarette instead and waited for Robert to finish. 'Well, they have no idea where he is,' he said, turning to her. 'Luc. Apparently he was *asked* to leave. Solange gave him a week's wages. Which was generous, considering. He had some boy in his room.'

'A boy?' The words escaped her as a shriek.

'He made a dreadful scene, she said. Really quite appalling. All this happened this morning. He was gone by noon.'

She sank back into her chair. 'Well, where does that get us, what does it have to do with anything?' At the same time she felt bad-tempered, and resentful of Daniel for giving her extra worry by the simple expedient of absenting himself from the disaster. Other, older rancours resurfaced: Daniel escaping England so that she had a double dose of maleficent parental interference to endure, and earlier still, Daniel evading punishments and unreasonable restrictions reserved for the first-born. Residual envy, sibling rivalry remain, the periods of favour not; for a child considers them no more than his due. And no more they are. Then the thought of their parents, their mother, made her miss him once more and fret quite selfishly for his company. 'I wish he'd call,' she said.

Robert said: 'Do you think there's something between them? I mean, between Daniel and that French boy?'

She stared at him. 'What on earth do you mean?'

He was embarrassed. 'He *is* your brother. I thought you might know. I thought he might have told you something.'

Rachel said: 'No, of *course* not. They were *friends*. Daniel explained it all to me. Luc made him laugh, took his mind off things.'

'What sort of things? What sort of things, Rachel?'

The telephone rang. 'If that's my mother tell her I've gone to bed, and that you're going too.'

But it was not her mother. Robert took the car and drove through the rain to the station. It was almost deserted at this hour, the last devoted commuters had passed through, and he saw Guy at once, standing in shadow next to the pay-phone from which he had made his call: Robert had to walk right across the station hall before Guy would step out from his shelter. 'A man gave me 10p to call you,' he said. 'He's gone now. You were a long time. Is Mummy here?'

'Mummy's waiting for you, she had to stay with Karl and Megan.' He put a hand on Guy's shoulder and propelled him towards the exit; the boy was dry and scarcely shiver-ing. As they walked Robert caught himself glancing into the corners and shadows of the station for some figure, some darker shadow watching their passage, even though Guy had said on the phone: 'Oh yes, I'm alone.'

'Where's Daniel then?' asked the boy, looking up at Robert.

'He's still in London. He'll be back later.' They paused in the station doorway. It was pouring with rain now, and he had parked the car on the other side of the road. 'Now when I say go, let's run for it' – as if they were braving sniper fire in some war-zone. They were soaked anyway. Guy slid into the passenger seat and belted himself in, and as Robert leaned over him to lock the passenger door he was aware of the boy's involuntary stiffening. They drove along and Robert murmured various comforting things. 'We'll get you home . . . we'll get you dry . . . we'll get you to bed . . .'

And it was as much to comfort himself that he spoke. For he loved Guy, loved him deeply – not with the broad, benevolent love he felt for Karl and Megan, so recognisably his own children in their bright, resilient earthiness. Guy was not his son, and Robert loved him with the nervous wakefulness of a responsibility assumed, something foreign and unlooked-for in his life. It was the same love he had extended, once and for all, to Rachel. But he knew that his part here was that of a simple functionary, ferrying the child over the last few leagues to his real homecoming.

Guy was sighing heavily, every ten seconds or so, as if from some constriction of the chest. Finally the white sliver of his face turned to Robert. 'Is Mummy very angry? She was crying on the phone.'

Robert stared ahead at the swimming windscreen and found he was nearly crying himself. 'She was just very happy to hear you. Sometimes people do that, you know, they cry because, well, because they're very happy. It doesn't always mean you've done something wrong.'

Guy considered this. Then tentatively, experimentally, he said: 'I cried, you know. The first night I cried so much I couldn't get to sleep.'

Panicking, Robert said with feigned heartiness: 'Look, old chap, you don't have to tell me anything, not till we get you home and into something warm. You can tell us all about it in the morning if you like. You must be dead tired . . .'

'Oh, I'*m* all right.'

Rachel had made some tea and sandwiches. They went into the living room where at last she held her son for a long time. Then she took him upstairs to put him in pyjamas and a dressing-gown. Robert was nursing a whisky when they returned. He said: 'Don't you want me to call your mother, let her know he's all right?'

'Not now,' said Rachel, more testily than she intended. 'She'd just ask questions.'

Guy only wanted milk. Again he asked: 'Where's Daniel? Is he really coming back tonight?'

'Tonight or tomorrow, darling. He'll be very glad to see you.'

And then, without any prompting, the boy told them what had happened. 'It was on Tuesday. You know I told you I went to the park with Jamie? Well, it wasn't true, Jamie was off school. I went to the cake shop in Dean Street, just to look. I was standing in front of the window and then there was a man standing next to me, and he said, which cake do you want? Well, I didn't want to talk to him, but I

145

said it didn't matter in any case which one I wanted because I didn't have any money, and I was just going when he said he bet he knew which one I'd choose, I'd choose a coffee éclair because it was my favourite. Then he said he knew my name was Guy Phillips and that he knew Robert and also Daniel, which seemed pretty likely because he spoke like a foreigner and Daniel knows a lot of foreigners.

'The man? Well, he was tall, about like Robert, and the same age, maybe a bit older. He had really dark hair and really dark eyes. He was wearing a suit and a big thick coat, which made him look quite big, fat, until he took it off. He had glasses on a chain, he put them on his nose and took them off again all the time. He smiled a lot. He was wearing a lot of perfume. And he talked in a foreign way.

'So he said we could go into the cake shop and have some cakes and something to drink, and that he wanted me to take a message, from him to you. And he said I could earn some money at the same time. And I was thinking that there couldn't be anything wrong, with him knowing Robert and Daniel like that, and so we went inside and he let me choose some cakes, and the odd thing was, he waited until I'd picked mine and then he chose exactly the same ones. And he got some coffee and I got a hot chocolate, and we found a table.'

So Guy had sat with the man in the tearoom and they had talked of this and that and Guy had eaten his cakes, and every so often the man had given some indication of how well he knew the family, such as the make and colour of Robert's car, or the name of the town in Yorkshire where Guy's grandmother lived, and all this while he left his own plate untouched. 'All of a sudden he said, "I'm not hungry, why don't you have these?" and he pushed his plate across the table. Then he told me not to say anything to anyone, but to meet him again, on Friday, after school, in the cake shop.'

Suddenly the boy was uncomfortable. Rachel said: 'Wait a minute, Guy. Just like that? He told you to go and meet him and you went? What about this message and this

146

money?' He was looking down at his hands. 'Oh darling, please, no one's going to be cross with you.'

'It's not that.' He reached for a tissue and blew his nose. 'Oh well. While we were sitting there he kept saying things he knew about me, and then he said that he – he knew that I took things, too. He said he knew that I'd taken things before, but that now I had a chance to take something and it would be all right, it would make up for all the times before. Everyone would be a winner, that's how he said it. He was really nice about it. I said, what do you mean? Then he described Daniel's watch to me. He said: "Have you seen something like that?" and I said yes, of course. He said: "And do you think you could get it for me?" And I said I didn't know. He said: "Well, you try and get that watch for me and bring it to me on Friday after school, and you'll get more than just a couple of cakes." I said what about Daniel? He said not to worry, Daniel wouldn't mind. He said: "And the watch belongs to me anyway." '

His face puckered and he began to cry noisily. 'I meant never to steal again. I promise I didn't want to. But he said: "You enjoy taking things, don't you?" And it wasn't true, really, but when he said it like that, somehow there was nothing I could do about it.'

She comforted him gently, with a copious supply of tissues. He blew his nose with finality and concluded, 'Then he said I could go. I said, what about the message? He winked at me and said: "*That's* the message." '

Then there was an interval of a few minutes where no one said anything. Robert got himself another drink, Guy sat patiently, pulling at the fringe of his dressing-gown cord, and Rachel thought about the man who had known that Guy stole.

'So,' she said at last, recollecting herself, 'you took Daniel's watch.'

'Yes. What could I do? And on Friday I went along to the cake shop – '

'– but there was no one there.'

He frowned at this interruption, and as if to reprimand

her paused before continuing. 'I waited ten minutes maybe, then I couldn't wait any longer, because I didn't have any money. So I started walking home. And when I turned off the main road a car pulled up, and there he was, in the car, driving, with another man in the back seat.' There followed a description of the car: a grey Volvo or something similar, newish, British number plates, right-hand drive. 'He let down the window and said he was sorry for being late. He said jump in and he'd take me home. I got in the car, the front seat. I said I'd got the watch and he asked to see it, and I can't remember anything after that.'

Rachel said wildly: 'What did they do to you?'

Guy bit his lip, fearful that her anger was directed against himself, that she thought he was lying or had earned all he got. 'I really don't know. I really don't know. Next thing, I was in a bed, feeling really sick. In fact I was. Sick.'

'Where was this?'

'On the floor.' Then he understood. 'In London. I didn't know it was London then. It was at the top of a big house, I know because the roof sloped a bit. It was early the next morning, I think, from the light. Somebody had put a bucket next to the bed but I didn't see it in time. So I think they knew I was going to be ill.'

And then he told them of the three days spent in the locked attic. 'It was like a flat. There was everything, a living room, a TV, a stereo. But I could only use it with the headphones, otherwise there was no sound at all. There were books and magazines, not really my sort of thing, you know, the magazines: suits and stuff. There was a little kitchen, just big enough to stand in, with a fridge packed with stuff. And a bathroom. And in the living room there was even another fridge like the one in the hotel in Brussels, with just drinks. But I didn't have any of those.' He was to mention again in the days to come how like a hotel it had been, the ultra-comfortable, antiseptic apartment at the top of a house in London.

A woman had appeared to clean up the mess and give him some thick white drink to calm his stomach. She came in twice or three times every day to heat up a pre-cooked lunch and dinner which she sat and ate with him. She was middle-aged and quite friendly, but appeared to speak no English: Guy thought she might have been Spanish or Italian. On the second day he made himself sick again, from over-eating he claimed, though Rachel suspected inroads made on the mini-bar, and the foreign woman had been very kindly, cleaning him up over and over again and sitting with him until he fell asleep. She seemed to be always on hand somewhere in the building, and to know when he needed something. His original plan, he explained, was to make himself so ill they would have to take him to a hospital or at least call a doctor, but the woman's ministrations had made it impossible. The rest of the time, when he was not eating or being ill, he watched television or cried. He started one of the books, he said, but couldn't get into it.

'And Daniel's watch?'

'Oh, I never saw that again.'

The first morning was dreadful, he recalled, a blur of panic and then weakness from being sick. In the afternoon he waited for something to happen and gingerly explored his new surroundings, and became very bored in the evening when he couldn't sleep. The next day had been passed in sickness. On the third day, that morning, someone else had come to see him with the foreign woman, a man, younger than the first and not so nice, Guy felt, though he had made every effort to appear friendly. 'He said in the evening I'd be able to come home, he said everything was "resolved". All I had to do was wait patiently and eat the food they gave me and not make a fuss and not make myself ill again. He said I'd been very good and deserved an award.'

'A reward?' suggested Rachel.

'No, I'm sure he said "award". Then he gave me a whole bunch of comic books, they were a bit stupid, full of puzzles and stuff. And he'd brought some films up for me and he showed me how to work the video. He asked me what my favourite food was and I said spaghetti bolognese because I couldn't think of anything else, and when the fat woman came back that's what she made and that's what we had for lunch. The man came again and asked me if everything was all right. He said I'd be going home in the evening and that I should have a shower and get properly clean, and he gave me my clothes back. Oh yes, I forgot to say: I was sick all over my clothes too the first day, and they took them away and gave me a sort of tracksuit to wear, and some pyjamas. They must have washed my clothes. In the afternoon the first man came, the one from the cake shop, with some more films. He asked me to choose one and when it was over I'd be able to go home. Just before the end all three of them came up. The woman stayed behind in the flat and the two men took me downstairs, through the house. I wanted to ask if I could phone you, but I was too scared they might change their minds and not let me go. I didn't see much of the house, just the staircase and the hall and a room where someone had left the door open. But it was an incredible house, with huge pictures everywhere on the walls like in a museum, and chandeliers, and huge vases on the floor. And the hall . . .'

'You don't know where you were?'

'No. The street was ordinary, just houses, but really grand ones. Well, I had to wait in the hall with the first man for a few minutes, and then we went outside. The second man was waiting in the car, and this time we got in the back. We drove to Paddington Station, it took about half an hour. I had my eyes closed all the time because I was pretending to be asleep. We stopped right in front of the station and the first man got out and went inside, and a few minutes later he came back and said: "Here is a train ticket and ten pounds. Your train leaves in five minutes from Platform Eight, so when you get out of the car you'd better run as fast as you can and not look back, or you'll miss your train." And that's what I did.' He was silent for a moment. 'The ten pounds is upstairs, in my pocket. I didn't want to spend it. I suppose I should give it to Daniel. After all, I took his watch.'

He was very tired by now. Rachel said: 'You can stay with me tonight, if you like. Robert can sleep in the spare room.' When Guy had padded off to the bathroom she said: 'Maybe we should have left all this till the morning.'

'No,' said Robert. 'He really needed to tell us.' He wanted to telephone the police straight away, but Rachel said: 'Be careful what you tell them for the moment. I don't want Daniel to get into trouble. Let's wait until we've heard what Daniel has to say.'

The next morning Robert went late to his office. 'Call me,' he said, turning at the door, 'if you want me for anything at all. I can be home in half an hour.' Guy, gratifyingly cheerful after a long sleep, was already playing with the younger children, who for their part were enchanted to see him.

Later, when Karl and Megan were having their afternoon naps, she was able to ask those questions which had come to stir within her during the night as Guy lay sleeping against her body. 'Did they talk to you? Did this man want anything from you? Did they give you any idea why you were there?'

'At first they only wanted to know if I was all right; if I had enough to eat, that sort of thing. If there was something special I wanted. I said I wanted some Marmite, and half an hour later the lady came in with a jar of Marmite, except I don't think they knew what to do with it, they just gave me the jar, and I had to ask if I could have some toast. Then today the man, the older one, asked me a lot of questions. He was quite friendly about it, he said he was just interested. He asked me about Grandma, about Robert's job, where we went for holidays. But I think he really wanted to know about Daniel. He asked if Daniel had any special friends, and I said yes, the French boy, but he said, apart from him. And so I mentioned Kristina and he wanted to know about her, what she looked like and where she lived and how long they'd known each other. Well, I couldn't tell him much. And they asked me what Daniel did with his days, and if he liked his job, and if he had shown us any photographs from when he was abroad.

And who he talked about. And if he was happy. And whatever I said, whatever I answered, he seemed very pleased. When he'd finished asking questions he said thank you, that it had been very interesting talking to me, and he gave me a bag full of chocolates and stuff, Mars bars and so on. But I didn't eat any. Mummy, has Daniel gone away?'

There was no sign from Daniel all that day, and by evening Rachel was convinced of a link between his departure and Guy's return. Was it for this he had felt unable to leave her a message of any kind? What, in the end, did she really know about her brother? And she refused to dwell on his absence, embracing instead her relief that Guy was back and so little scarred by what he had been through.

Of course this was in appearance only. Though he chose to sleep in his own room that night, he woke her sometime after three, standing wan and forlorn at her bedside. They went downstairs and he lay on the sofa with his head in her lap, as of old, while she stroked his hair. He couldn't say what was disturbing him, didn't even attempt to describe the dreams that had woken him. But she looked down at his eyelids, which would flutter closed for a moment and then swiftly open, and thought she knew. And briefly she understood that he would never be wholly hers again, after those three days among strangers, dependent on their kindness and calling on their comfort, accepting the food they offered, thankful for the ministrations they tendered, and huntedly aware that this kindness was not ingenuous, this comfort not disinterested, that the one need never have been offered and the other might yet be withdrawn. He knew that he was fortunate to be alive, and this was the beginning of adult knowledge. It requires real innocence to refuse the mercies of strangers: Guy was not so innocent. He had agreed to live amongst them, and a part of him would live there always, guilty, grateful, and terrified, with a mouthful of cake and a stolen wristwatch in his pocket, mortgaged to another's conditional hospitality.

11

A Case of the Past

Daniel didn't return. Rachel no longer counted him in for meals; his name dropped from their conversations, which were in any case resolutely oriented towards the future. Guy didn't ask about him, understanding obscurely that his safe restitution had been bought at the price of Daniel's absence. He was not forgotten, it was simply felt that his name was an ill omen and his return something they should not hope for. Rachel found herself avoiding the room that had been his, just as a few days earlier she had hurried past the door to Guy's room, unable to face the emptiness within. Lawrence the cat had taken to slinking in there at odd moments, scenting abandoned territory: when Rachel finally summoned the courage to brave the room one day she found the animal lying, in solitary possession, on Daniel's bed. As for Karl, if he ever wondered aloud where Daniel could be, Rachel gave the same answers, vague and reassuring, and besides, Karl's memory was blessedly short.

She thought with amazement of those days when Guy was missing. It seemed she had passed through them with the mute numbness of a sleepwalker or a character in a dream. Where had it been, all the fear, the hysteria? She remembered odd moments of lucidity when she had been quite able to perform mundane, everyday tasks: mending, washing clothes, when she had felt odd, displaced worry, about Daniel, about Megan's health – for all the world as if the world were not coming to an end. Am I a monster, she wondered, to have felt so little? Or had she dimly understood more than she knew? Now, with Guy restored to her, she began to feel it all, merciful days later, as when beneath a fading anaesthetic there pulses into life the pain of the incision, the throb of healing.

With Guy she had sudden losses of control. The school had agreed to his being kept at home for the last two weeks of term – were grateful, in fact, to be spared this one additional problem; even so, with him there in the house and disinclined to venture into the rainy outdoors, even so she knew no peace, and would suddenly lay down her dishes or drop her needlework and hurry to the room where he was reading, or else she would push ajar his door to catch the sound of his breathing in the night. They went out to choose Christmas presents and she was appalled at the numbers of people, all this promiscuous access in the genteel thoroughfares of the town, the ease with which a child might be abducted or simply won away. Standing there with him in the eddy of the pedestrian street she was unable to move for fear. 'Mummy, do you know you're hurting me?' he asked, embarrassed. She gave a nervous laugh as, looking down, she realised with just what ferocity she had been gripping his arm. He, meanwhile, would not look at her, understanding too well the cause of her fear and recognising his own responsibility.

The subject of Brussels, in abeyance for the duration of the crisis, resurfaced. Shamefaced over dinner one evening Robert told her that he would have to give an answer before Christmas. 'Only if you're absolutely sure,' he said. 'I don't want to uproot us all again.' A great core of loneliness hollowed itself out within her at the thought, and then came surprise at how much of this was because, whichever way she chose, Daniel would not be there.

Next day she went to his room, which was just as he had left it. His dressing-gown lay across one corner of the bed, and, picking it up to hang on the back of the door, she was conscious of the symbolic finality of the gesture. Somehow it became important to continue the process, and she stripped down the bed and carried the sheets through to the

154

linen-basket; she arranged the scattered books and cassettes, setting aside those she herself might read or listen to in the days to come. But his cardigan she put aside with revulsion, as if it were salvage. It was true that he had brought trouble into their lives: even so she could feel no resentment towards her brother. In a sense she had wished it on herself when she envied him all his own troubled past.

She toyed with the idea that she had let him down. But seeing beyond the six years' gap that separated them and the memory of all the times he had been left with her as a child, she knew that this teasing out of a maternal instinct was a part of Daniel's charm and armoury, searching after surrogate mothers the length of this and other countries. At his school, at university, likewise she supposed abroad, he had always courted the mothers along with the sons, often growing away from his friends as he grew ever more the intimate of their houses, winning the older women's devotion with his well-spoken helplessness and sexless gallantry. She supposed that he had made use of this little-boy-lost air in order to make use of the women: she too could have felt used. But she guessed that Daniel's cultivation of appearances was entirely instinctual to him and thus, with the desperate honesty of self-preservation, altogether natural, as an impounded animal under sentence of destruction will know to make itself adorable to the eyes of a potential master.

'I can't help but think it would never have happened if Daniel hadn't gone to live with you,' commented their mother with her diabolical intuition.

Rachel was all the quicker to defend him, given her new-found certainty that the accusation was true. 'Danny had nothing to do with it,' she said, 'he loves Guy.' As she spoke she turned, cradling the receiver, to where Robert sat, and raised her eyes heavenward.

The voice crackled back down the line. 'He's bad news,' said Mrs Marriner. 'He grew away from us, he never cared about the family. He was bad for the children; look what he did to Guy. Look at the way he just left without a word.' She sighed. 'I suppose I can always tell myself that once I *had* a son. Thank God I've still got my grandchildren. When are you going to bring them up to see us? Poor little Guy!'

Something cracked inside Rachel. 'Do you think Guy doesn't remember how you were with him when he was small? Do you think Karl won't remember? And Megan, too, when it's her turn? In a few years they'll be making up their own minds, deciding for themselves whether they come and visit you, whether they want to see you. And if they decide that no, they don't, they'd really rather be somewhere else, will you be surprised? And hurt? Will you write them off the way you've written Danny off now?'

She was shaking as she slammed the receiver, as Robert led her to the sofa and sat her down. Wearily she knew that she would pay for her outburst, that the next hour she would be feeling guilty, the hour following anxious, that tomorrow she would have to call her mother to apologise. She could not defend Daniel for much longer, when her own children stood in need of such protection. They would regain their precedence with her, struggling as they must against their apportioned burden of that guilt bequeathed down the generations. Already it was beginning to show in Guy, in his reluctant subterfuges, his furtive thefts, his shame at his own abduction.

She had an image of the chain that united and bound them all. Mother and daughter both, she was a link in that chain even as she was its prisoner, bound by the same patterns of guilt and failure which are as essential and potent a part of intricate heredity as the make-up of genes determining that a child shall be left- or right-handed, have blue eyes and blonde hair, a predilection for music or mathematics, a preference for playing with little girls rather than little boys. The chain bound her as it formed her, just as it had bound and formed their mother and doubtless *her* mother, and on and on, into the unspeakable past; and, timeless and infinitely self-regenerating, it would tighten around and inside her until she regretted her words of this evening.

She saw them, her ancestors, locked in their attitudes

of guilt and punition as in some purgatorial stained-glass tableau, the afflicted, averted faces of the dead mothers and sons. Perhaps after all she need not join them; perhaps her momentary defiance had been a first step, a straining at the chain, a refusal to submit to and pass on their heavy bequest. Perhaps tomorrow she would find it that bit easier. It would take work, hard work, a lifetime's: well, there was no place in all of that for Daniel. Beside whatever road or in whosever room, he was beyond the scope of love and her loneliness: she could no more work to protect him in his absence than elect to live his life for him. She would have to forget Daniel, the better to remember herself and her own. She told herself that when all was said and done they were his choices to make, his errors to commit and amend, his dangers to surmount or succumb to, his life to live, his chain to break. And so they were, and so it is.

Into the relative peace of the late wintry evening came Luc. Robert started at the doorbell and said: 'Daniel.' But 'No,' said Rachel, rising from her chair with odd certainty, 'it couldn't be Daniel, he has his own key.'

Luc stood there on the doorstep with that lopsided smile, and with a drink-lit nimbus about him that gauzed his eyes and gave a blurry weight to his face. For all his corrupt loveliness he looked rather bedraggled and urchin-like: an old raincoat, clearly not his own, hung over his waiter's shirt and black pants; the shirt collar was patterned with tiny blood spots from shaving.

'I lost my job,' he announced, his breath misting in the cold air as if his every emanation must take on a manifest physical nature. It was then that she noticed the bag slung over his shoulder. 'They threw me out of the hotel.'

'What do you want?' she said. 'Daniel isn't here, you know.' Still she held onto the door.

'I heard,' he said nonchalantly. Then: 'It's late, I know.'

They faced each other for a moment. 'You'd better come

in then.' He stumbled slightly on the threshold and cursed under his breath in his own language. 'Are you all right?' she asked, rather annoyed.

'Too much whisky, I guess. It helps keep out the cold. When you're out on the streets . . .'

'Oh yes?' she said. 'The streets?' He followed her through to the living room. 'Robert, look,' she said. 'It's Daniel's friend.'

Luc laid down his bag, removed his coat, glanced around the room. 'Nice place,' he said, quite as if he had never been there. He stood for a moment in front of the Christmas tree. 'Nice tree.' He turned and waited.

Robert was looking at him hard. 'Look,' he said to Rachel, not taking his eyes off the visitor, 'I don't want this boy in my house.'

'I am disturbing you?' said Luc.

'I don't want him in my house. Haven't we had enough trouble as it is?'

Rachel was standing between them. She stepped towards her husband, as if to indicate where her allegiances ultimately lay. 'Robert,' she said softly.

He looked from one to the other. Then he rose, gathered up the papers that had drifted from the arm of his chair to the floor, and said: 'Oh well, please yourself. Whatever it is, just try to get it over and done with quickly, all right?'

'Robert!' she called out after him. Then, turning to Luc: 'I was going to make some coffee. D'you want some?'

'I think I maybe stick to whisky, if you don't mind.' Catching her expression, he added: 'It's okay, I brought my own.' He undid the zipper of his bag and brought out a bottle half-full. 'Please. It's for you, too.'

'I think I'd prefer coffee.'

He grinned. 'Got to go and comfort your old man?' She gave him a look of such undiluted venom that he said hastily: 'I'm sorry. This is really good of you, you know.'

In the kitchen Robert stood, leaning heavily on the breakfast bar. 'Are you quite sure about this?'

Steadily, Rachel said: 'No. No, I'm not sure. It's just . . . Well, if I don't, I never *will* be sure, will I?'

'Solange said he was wild at the hotel, that morning he left. She thinks he's mad. I'm just asking you to be careful.'

Luc already had a glass of whisky next to him when she returned with her coffee. He was sprawled on the floor with his arms outstretched along the sofa behind him, and she had barely sat down in her own chair when he began. 'They threw me out of the hotel. Some old cow of a cleaner saw Jason coming out of my room real early. We weren't hurting anybody. After that I had to sleep rough, you know?' He gave her a sideways look to catch her reaction. 'Well, I guess I only slept out that first night. Then I took a train down to London and stayed with some friends.'

She attempted to keep her voice light. 'Lucky you had these friends.'

He was indignant. 'Well, what was I supposed to do? I tried to find Jason, I went to his house, all the way up in Hampstead. Those guys, they had money, I never saw a house like it. They had dogs, they had some kind of an electric gate. Am I going to walk up there, dressed like this, knock on their door? You can guess the reception I'd get. So I go to the club, right? Where I met Jason, you know, that night with Danny. So I'm thinking, maybe he'll show up there again. But he didn't. Only I met some other guys.' He paused, then smirked up at her. 'I draw a veil. Next day, I call up Jason, only he isn't there, he doesn't live there at all, it's a phoney number he's given me, phoney address.' He took a great gulp of whisky and almost choked on it. Then, quite without warning, he began to cry, drily, without real tears. 'So where am I going to look for him in this city? All I've got is clubs, streets on streets of clubs, the only addresses I had.' He calmed down somewhat and stared glumly into his drink. 'Not that I blame him, mind you. Phoney address, phoney number, phoney name maybe for all I know: well, it's not like I never did it myself. You don't go round telling strangers who you are and where to find you. But Jesus Christ, I wish I could see him again.'

He fell silent and morose. The hysteria, that darker side to his fearless, life-giving hilarity, was averted for the present. But the tears he had made as if to cry a moment ago were dried up at the source, somewhere back in his hard-faced, hard-bargained youth, and crying now must have been as painful to him as retching on an empty stomach. Luc knew the desolation, even as he knew its value, of many years of self-control. As for Rachel, already regretting her coldness of a moment ago, if the spectacle of his distress had upset her enough, quite awful was the bruised smile he managed for her now as he said: 'So there we are then. Just one more bastard.'

'Luc,' she said quietly, leaning forward. 'Luc, what did they do to Guy?'

It shocked him out of his introspection. 'He *is* back, isn't he?' Then, relaxing: 'For a second back there I thought something might have gone wrong.'

She stared at him, then laughed out loud in her angry disbelief. 'My, you really are something. You sit there, on my floor, and you really don't see that there's any difference between a child who gets kidnapped and locked in a room for four days, and the fact that some trashy teenager has done a runner on you.'

He said, with another sideways look: 'As a matter of fact the two stories have a lot in common.' But she was not amused. 'I'm sorry,' he said. 'You're mad at me.' He slopped more whisky into his glass, waved the bottle towards her. 'Have a shot of this, it'll make you feel better.'

'I don't want any.'

'Have some,' he said with surprising sharpness. There was a moment of silence. He continued more softly: 'I hate drinking alone, I really can't stand it. I have to have somebody drink with me.' He stood up, took a glass from the trolley, poured out some whisky and placed it in her unresisting hand.

She looked down at it, laughed again, and drank. 'And that's the only thing that matters, isn't it? *You* can't stand to drink alone, so *I* have to have some whisky.'

He resumed his place on the floor. 'Everyone expects me to be so wise, that's the trouble.'

'Believe me, that's not my opinion of you at all.'

'Oh it is, you know,' he said simply. 'Everyone expects me to be so wise, and have all the answers, and be tough, and take all the knocks. That's what Danny thinks, and he's had long enough to learn better. But it suits him, it's something he can depend on. Well, you want to know the truth? I throw out a good line, is all.'

Suddenly she was glad of the whisky. 'Poor misunderstood Luc. How much did you have to do with this business with Guy?'

'Hey, I'm not a *gangster*.' He grinned up at her; still she did not smile. 'Truly. I didn't know what was going on. I didn't click to as how big this thing had got, I never reckoned as how it might involve you and the little boy. My instructions were to get Danny back, simply that. The business with the little boy, that was something else again, that was bad.' She remained silent. 'Look, I know I've been a stupid kid and I guess I don't come out of all this too well. But it's over. Believe me. Cross my heart. It's over now.'

She lifted her face. 'And Daniel? He's gone for good? He won't be back?'

'Well, don't hold your breath. Course, it was all because of the little boy, you must have guessed that much. When Danny found out that he had gone, that's when he knew the game was up. That he'd have to go back. He wouldn't have thought twice about it. He's a good kid really.' Then, seeing her puzzlement: 'Daniel, I mean.' He said: 'No, no, he won't be coming back. How could he, after all this? And what would he be coming back for anyway, please? There's nothing for him in this country. Oh, there's you, yes – he was very fond of you.'

'Thank you,' she said tonelessly.

He sat there, nursing his whisky, calmly informing her about this brother of hers as if she had hardly known him. And, she reasoned, he was right, he knew far more than she, and what he didn't know could guess. And so she listened

161

obediently while Luc told her about Daniel. 'Yes, he's gone back to Paris, but I can't say for how long. After that it's anywhere Carlos decides to take him. There's always a place for him in Paris, but, you know, Carlos isn't too keen on Paris and he doesn't let Danny stay there long. I guess they'll be doing a bit of travelling around now, to keep Danny out of trouble. Tell you the truth, I don't think Danny cares overmuch where he is anymore.

'Carlos: that isn't his real name, that's what we called him, Danny and me and a few others. I thought I knew his name but apparently *that's* not the real one either. For sure Danny knows it now, but I'm not reckoning on seeing Danny again.

'Carlos gives him plenty of freedom, you don't have to worry about that. It's really not such a bad ticket, considering what Danny *could* have ended up with. Considering the state he was in at the time. He can do his own thing for weeks at a throw, travel around, visit people, shuttle between Nice and Paris if he wants to, spend all day on a beach and all night in a club, if that's the way he's feeling. There's times I for one wouldn't turn it down. He can go picking up every girl who walks down the Promenade des Anglais if he wants, and I guess there's a good bit of that, too. Carlos goes in for some weird stuff.

'Maybe you've got the idea Carlos watches over him like a hawk. That Carlos: he *couldn't* be watching Danny, not with the life he leads. But man, don't let Danny stray too far too long – Carlos'll have him back with one short whistle. That was their deal. Danny didn't understand it. Or maybe he just forgot. And that's what all this is about: Danny strayed too far, and Carlos decided to give the whistle.

'So he found out where Danny was and what he was doing and who he was living with. He already had a few people out here, they did his groundwork for him. And then *I* was called up. And you know, I needed a break and I missed Danny, and I figured as how I could use the ticket, and there were a few people I was trying to steer clear of in France. And they gave me a bit of money, and I reckoned as

162

how it was nothing too shady, just to check up on Danny and report back once in a while and maybe make Danny see that he couldn't jack it all in like that. There was no mention of the kid – your kid.

'I was surprised when Carlos didn't act sooner. But apparently after I arrived in England he called off his watchdogs here and was quite content to let me bum along in my own way. He didn't even show any interest those times when I called to report back. 'Course, it wasn't him I spoke to. I thought maybe as how he'd given up the whole idea: given up on Danny, I mean. Maybe he was just busy someplace else. But I guess one day he must just have decided okay, that's enough, now Danny comes home. And he gave the whistle. Which was your little boy.

'By the way. There was no connection between them taking Guy when they did and our going down to London. It was bad luck, the way it happened, it held up the whole proceedings. If Danny had been here when they grabbed the kid maybe you'd have got him back a whole lot quicker.'

He looked up at her and spoke with a greater urgency. 'Don't you notice the way Danny is sometimes? So smiling, so nice, always goes along with whatever you say. And you'll be talking to him quite merrily and he'll answer you and a minute later you realise it's like he's been in someone else's conversation? He's acting it's like a part of his brain has been cut out? Let me tell you about Danny. The truth is, Danny is strictly the kind of guy where – and I've *seen* this happen – he will sit in a restaurant staring at his chequebook while he figures out what name to sign. 'Cause a part of his brain *has* been cut out. And he wanted it that way.

'He was so frightened. That boy was scared of everything! My guess is, he came to Paris to bomb out. He was running away, okay, but that kid had such a bad case of the past he didn't even know what he was running from. He was a junkie, but he was like any kind of a junkie: drugs, drink, sex – didn't matter what so long as he could get bombed out on it. Sleep, even. Anything to kill whatever it was in his head. *You* must know what happened when he was a kid that fucked him up like this.

'And that's where Carlos came in. I guess Danny's head was so messed up that even with all his bombing out he still couldn't get clear of it. And he was so full of guilt and stuff that it was just getting worse, all this falling asleep on stairs in nightclubs, waking up in weird hotels or on some highway miles out of town – it was getting *sinister*. And so he sold his soul. It sounds crazy, I know, but that's what he did. Sold it. Or maybe just gave it away. And all he asked in return was someone to pick him off the floor and pay for a taxi and get him enough drugs when he was feeling bad until it went away again, and take him to swish places where he could pick up dumb girls or whatever he was into picking up that particular week, and generally just tell him what to do.'

'But there's one thing I don't understand,' said Rachel. 'Why did he come back to England if he hated it here so much?'

'Oh, beats me, what would I know? He's so full of guilt and lies. Same question I asked him, I heard a dozen answers. One day he tells me, in all seriousness: "All those years abroad I was running away, now I've stopped running." ' He was pulling at his fringe. Now he looked up at her, shrugged, and smiled. 'Truth is, it doesn't happen like that. *You* can try and junk the past, the problem is other people. Like, you've got a debt? – it'll follow you round the world. And then you're running away from running away, and on and on. Did he really think he could dump us all like that?'

The whisky bottle had emptied as he talked on and to Rachel it seemed that this latter half of his story was addressed less to her than to the glass he swirled round and round, gazing into its deep, unfathomable companionship. Now he got up and took Robert's whisky from the trolley and unscrewed the top with a careful and quite steady hand.

He said: 'I know the kind of life he's going back to and,

frankly, it's not too bad. He's happy enough, or at least he will be, with his Walkman and his music and his new clothes, and his cafés and his glasses of wine and his girls on the seafront at Nice. Like I said, he doesn't much care where he is any more. It's not such a bad life, and at least it's safer than what he was doing before.'

Rachel was softly crying. 'It sounds awful.'

'You think so?' He looked up at her, the alcoholic gauze lifting momentarily from his eyes to reveal the detention of terrible knowledge. 'You think so? There's plenty would envy him.'

She felt the nagging duty to find out more about this Carlos, what manner of man he was that could exercise such power, marshal and distribute such forces here and in his own country. But greater was the desire not to know him, this man who had forced his way once already into her life, her living room: banal as it was and homely, she preferred to keep its door closed against him now. And so she laid down her glass and remembered Daniel as he had been in those early and untroubled weeks, if the lack of trouble were not illusion alone. 'I'll miss him,' she said, 'really I will. I didn't know him as well as you, but I got to love him in a way. The children, too. I hope he'll be all right.'

'Don't you worry,' said Luc. He smiled at her almost shyly. She opened her mouth to answer him, but in the end said only: 'I'm going to make some more coffee.' Indicating the bottle: 'I suppose you're sticking with that?'

'No, I think I'll have coffee too, if that's okay. I can drink so much, then it's time for a coffee. If I have some coffee, then I'm okay.'

Robert was seated at the breakfast bar, reading a report whilst spooning breakfast cereal into his mouth. 'He still here?'

'I'll get rid of him in a minute. He can drink his coffee and then go.'

But when she came back to the living room he was out cold, his head lolling against his shoulder and one arm thrown out across the floor. She called Robert and together they lifted him onto the sofa. She pulled off his shoes and then went in search of something to cover him with, returning a moment later. He lay there and she stood in front of him, her arms filled with the duvet Daniel had used. He resembled a painting; he looked like *The Death of Chatterton* or some such artist's version of another artist – stylised, perfected, an image of himself rather than a self: Luc, the Marvellous Boy.

She cleared away the bottle, the glasses, the ashtrays, while Robert carried the tray with the three coffee cups still on it, up to their bedroom. 'Quarter to two,' she said. 'I hope he'll be all right down there.'

Her husband paused in his undressing and put a hand on her shoulder. 'I thought I should tell you,' he said, 'I said no to Brussels.'

Megan woke her next morning shortly after seven. She paused at the head of the staircase on hearing Luc's voice below, speaking into the phone. '*Oui, maman,*' he was saying. '*Oui, maman.*' An ugly, desperate catch entered his voice. '*Non, maman, bien sûr que non.*' And then a long silence as the other spoke, and: '*Oui, maman. Au revoir, maman, je t'embrasse.*' Rachel waited there for a moment with Megan quiet and puzzled in her arms.

When she reached the door of the kitchen Luc was there, holding a carton of orange juice, clean, bright, his skin glowing like some miracle of endurance and renewal in the early light. He had about him that air of owning the place, which was as near as ever he would come to possessions or home. Nearby sat Guy, engrossed in a book of puzzles, already quite won over to the situation.

Luc was wearing her apron; he smiled at her broadly.

'Good morning. We've been up for ages. I've made you breakfast.'

'Good morning,' she answered, and stepped into the room.

12

Staying for Breakfast

Daniel sat in the brasserie called Galaxie in the Gare du Nord and tried to remember when he had been there last. He thought perhaps another beer might help him, and summoned the waiter. Around the station, camped in corners, huddled around stairs, were hundreds of young travellers like himself, like himself at least in so far as they were young – sitting, standing, lying even, some of them, as they waited for the night trains to other countries of Europe: with well-worn foam mattresses rolled into their backpacks, cans of beer and bottles of water, hasty picnics prepared for the journey ahead of baguette, supermaket pâté: subsistence food. The girls with hair unwashed, the men stubbly, they waited in the gratifying fatigue of a shoestring odyssey drawing to a close.

Much of the concourse was boarded off for the renovation work in progress: another few months and the station would be unrecognisable. He had been sitting in almost the same place, he remembered, with the same voluminous bag on the ground beside him. But it had been summer then, morning, warm: he had not required a coat. There had been a reason for his sitting there. The departure, yes, of course that – but something else. He had been expecting someone, someone who wanted to say goodbye. He resolved to wait for his beer and only then turn his mind to the problem.

The waiter returned with the drink and set it down before him. Daniel looked up and nodded in a friendly way, slightly puzzled that the man continued to hover there, over his table. Only when he heard the man repeat, '*Douze francs, s'il vous plaît*', did he realise he was being asked to settle at once. He took a handful of unfamiliar counters from his pocket and laboriously put the sum together. On the boat, at customs, again in the train pulling out of Dunkerque, he had scarcely noticed the fact of French being spoken all about him, as if the captain's announcements and the commands of the passport controllers were mere international verbal gestures, beyond place or language, requiring no special effort of response; and his own drinks, here in Paris, he had ordered with a mechanical uninterest in what was on offer or what he might actually want. Now, with the waiter's face creasing impatiently above him, he heard himself stammer out two or three words of apology, then, like the springing lock of an old casket, the language clicked open inside him. He launched into an elaborate, self-deprecating explanation, the waiter smiled, reassured, and Daniel knew he would be able to function here again, more or less.

Luc. It was Luc he had been meeting all those months ago, Luc who had stood by the gate to Platform 11, reading a newspaper, smoking a cigarette, Luc he had waved to, called out for. Luc had crossed the station, slipped into the seat beside him; they had laughed and joked about the forthcoming departure. 'In any event,' Luc had said, 'I'll be seeing you again soon, in England.' Luc had helped him with his luggage, accompanied him as far as the train. Luc had given him a watch.

He looked down at his wrist and remembered with immense sadness that it had not been Luc that morning, here on the so-called terrace of the Brasserie Galaxie in the Gare du Nord four months ago. Who then could have given him the watch? An expensive one, Swiss, gold: it had been no ordinary watch. And with effort at last he recalled Saskia, Carlos' one-time wife and later procuress, Saskia who had presided over so many wonderful parties all that famous first summer on the Côte d'Azur, Saskia who had sat with him, the last morning, shivering in her fabulous fur coat although it was only September, while he brushed the flakes of ash from the tips of her hair. Daniel looked down at his wrist; the pale band of skin where the watch had been was already almost faded away.

Finishing his beer rather quickly, he took a taxi to the Parc Monceau, way over in the expensive west of Paris. Here there was someone to carry up his bag for him, someone to show him how to operate the television, the lights in the bathroom, the phone. He crossed to the window, leaned against the ice-cold wrought-iron grille, and watched for a moment the melancholy, yellow headlamps of cars speeding home to suburban families in these last few days before Christmas. He was alone in his rich, comfortable hotel room whose bill was someone else's concern; he was back in safekeeping. With resignation and an ironic sense of inevitability he made his way over to the mini-bar. The four months in England, the abstinence, the labour, the family – they had been the aberration, rather than this old life he had once managed to believe so glamorous, so dangerous and exciting. England had been the aberration, and all the while he had done no more than play at domesticity and calm, like Marie Antoinette amidst her sheep and her peasant furnishings. It was foolish to imagine that he might have continued indefinitely if only Luc had not appeared, ostensibly to visit his old friend, in fact to reclaim him for the shades. The mistake was in believing that his life was his own, that he could change it or take responsibility for it. Luc had been right to mock that quiet existence, buried in genteel rural Oxfordshire – tending the children, retiring ostentatiously to an early bed – as just one other trip.

In the mini-bar he found, alongside the customary cans and spirit miniatures, a bottle of Piper Heidsieck with a celebratory ribbon tied round its neck. Drawing the cork, pouring himself a glass with only minimal spillage of foam, he marvelled at his recovered strength and dexterity. He was back in the old life, no longer glamorous or exciting, if indeed it ever had been: now it was just life. As he drank, there stole over him a huge relief which was not that of an

169

alcoholic, deprived the whole day long, who takes his first lifegiving sips, for hadn't he gone without drink for months on end and suffered not unduly? It was not his body which shuddered now with pleasure so much as his mind, tired of the thankless effort of lucidity.

A bell rang in the room and he made his way to the door. 'Here is a package for Monsieur . . .' The bellboy was somewhere in his late teens, pretty in a sluttish sort of way beneath the stiffness of the uniform that creaked around his immature shoulders like a best Sunday suit raided from Father's wardrobe. For a second Daniel toyed with the idea of seducing him, of turning from the door, casually unbuttoning his shirt – 'Why don't you come in for a moment? I was just about to take a shower . . .' The guest in the foreign hotel, the serviceable adolescent: it was every cliché from every one of the interchangeable films he had watched together with Carlos and his company in the bored torpor of that last summer, films in which everybody was available, irrespective of age, sex, status or want. The bellboy was beginning to look uncomfortable as still Daniel did not take the proffered package. 'Why don't you make yourself at home. I'll join you in a second . . .' Daniel imagined the ungainly flush beneath the starched collar, the awkwardness, the worry for his job, and he knew he could not even be bothered with the boy, with trying to recall the rites, gestures, hypocritical assurances of seduction. He took the parcel and 'Go then, go,' he said, with unintended sharpness. 'Run along, now.'

Alone again, he opened the package. It was a small leather box containing the Raymond Weil watch. Without even glancing at the accompanying card he slipped on the watch and considered how handsome, how well-made and efficient, how expensive and well-bred it looked against his skin; and he thought how naked, immature and even childish his wrist had seemed without it. The gold deepened the memory of his summer tan; the exquisite Roman figures gave age, taste, experience to his otherwise anonymous flesh. He stretched out his arm and held it up to the light, there to admire the artificial perfection of the watch and his own, less durable perfection. At the same time, with that old irony, he acknowledged the symbolic implication of accepting the watch a second time, of slipping it on so gratefully and acquiescing so immediately to the dictates of its rhythm: already, he thought, already one wrist was shackled. But he had never had inculcated in him pride enough to refuse a gift.

He picked up the card. Beneath the time of the appointment and the name of a smart café at Saint Michel they had frequented a year ago, he read the laborious message: 'This is for you wont be Late: *Dont Lose it a second time!*' Poor Carlos: scarcely literate in English, in French little better. And yet it was touchingly personal, this note in Carlos' own painful hand, when he could so easily have had one of his minions write it, with grammatical precision and real menace in the warning. Welcome home, Daniel.

He lay down on the bed and stared at the new ceiling. So many ceilings over the years, so many hotels in cities with so many forgotten partners, so many beds in strange rooms which were not so strange to him. Indeed, the very strangeness was familiar, almost comforting. Nobody knew where he was, nobody expected anything of him.

The story of their first encounter had been told and retold and had entered the separate mythologies of both. It was Daniel's second full summer in France and he was hitting the end of a three-month binge which had somehow or other beached him on the Riviera with Luc and a local fast set. Luc it was who had prevailed on him to come along to the party, not that this required much doing, since Daniel at that time could be persuaded into more or less anything by more or less anyone. He was already pretty far gone, as indeed he had been through most of their week in Cap d'Agde, when at last the taxi deposited them in front of the floodlit villa, and Luc, ever lucid, grew swiftly bored and soon offloaded him on the terrace steps with a gaggle of rich kids, friends of Carlos' and Saskia's daughter. Saskia herself – since this was still early days and before the period of her own infatuation with Daniel – was none too pleased to see him, uninvited and out of control, in her house, and she went to considerable trouble to keep him out of Carlos' way even when Carlos, intrigued, wondered aloud who this new boy might be. In the event, Daniel predictably slunk off with his newfound friends straight after the midnight supper, to try some drug or other. He was in an hilarious mood that evening, he later heard.

They emerged from the house about a half hour later, by which time they were no longer by any means the rowdiest among the guests. Saskia's daughter thought it would be an excellent idea to go for a swim in the pool, around which the soberer guests still lounged over their weak cocktails and half-finished supper plates, and very soon the three boys and two girls, harshly laughing as if their lives depended on it, and barely able to keep upright, had stripped to their underclothes and jumped in. The second his abused body hit the emetic water Daniel's whole precarious euphoria evaporated. After a few minutes of casting about aimlessly, as if trying to work his clumsy limbs back into some semblance of coordination, he managed to pull himself up out of the pool, standing vaguely at its edge and trying to remember where he had put his clothes, and puzzled as to why he was shivering so violently. By this time Carlos had taken a judicious seat at one of the poolside tables, whence he looked up, as if in surprise, when Daniel limped past, dripping, over the lawn, across the deserted terrace, and deep into the house.

Carlos found him twenty minutes later in one of the downstairs bathrooms. The door was not locked. Daniel was lying unconscious alongside the toilet, into which he had unsuccessfully been trying to vomit. Carlos propped him into a sitting position and proceeded to clean him up with a cold flannel. When he was finished he called someone to help him carry the boy to his car, a second person to swab out the bathroom after them, a third to inform Saskia, briefly, of what had happened. It was swiftly, professionally,

172

and really quite humanely done. Carlos was an old hand at abduction.

Later, when he pictured the scene, Daniel was amazed anew that here were the beginnings of his year-long association with Carlos. He had never seen himself as one who required help or deserved kindness, but rather as an object of disgust better left where it was. How could Carlos, how could anyone, finding him like that, seeing him like that, have been moved to gather up his infantile limbs, kiss his slack and rancid mouth, smoothe his soaked hair? In the world that he knew there was no such indulgence, and, fatally, it never occurred to him that his own need might call forth affection in another. Need was something dirty and something to be punished for. Someone else's bathroom had been dirtied with his need. He could have no notion of what Carlos felt, standing in the doorway, taking in his awkwardly fallen shape, his shrunken flesh. And it was in very different terms that they would invoke and consider those armfuls of tenderness in the bathroom at Cap d'Agde. And though with time the evening became a source of amusement, an accident the memory of which lent a momentary extra closeness to their ordinary relations, it was in fact the first fissure of misconception on which those relations rested.

He had woken the next morning in a house whose surpassing luxury he didn't know, naked in a huge bed in a great white room with, some small way off, the Mediterranean making its quiet morning noise against the most expensive stretch of geology in Europe. The windows were open and the long curtains billowed pleasantly. Daniel turned his head from side to side and felt the linen give against his cheeks. His clothes, washed and pressed, were neatly folded over the back of a chair. So white and clean, so hushed and restful was it all that for a moment he wondered if he was not in some hospital: this wouldn't be the first time he had woken, with a splitting head and the aftertaste of catastrophe, in a hospital. But what institution looked so rich, smelt so unearthly hospitable? He lowered the sheet and looked down at his body, its undeserved health and wholeness, so many times bartered, so many times pledged. Swinging out of bed he caught sight of himself in a vast mirror. He moved up close, amazed with each step to find this face, which had passed through so many hands, unblemished, quite fresh, and recognisably his own.

He picked up his clothes and weighed their fine cleanliness in his hands, then dressed and let himself quietly out of the room. The house was still. He found a bathroom, wonderfully white, with thick carpets and thick towels. Downstairs there was a big salon, again in white, with soft couches and armchairs and a white grand piano, and a few inoffensive modern paintings. His impression was of a sanatorium contrived to reconcile its troubled inmates to the idea of heaven. He stepped out onto the terrace where, on a white wrought-iron table covered by a red and white trattoria-style cloth, his breakfast had been laid out for him with it seemed as much concern for decor as had gone into the provision of the improbably blue Mediterranean beyond. On the table were a basket of croissants under a white napkin, various containers of jams, a butter-dish, a carafe of orange juice, a pot of coffee, a jug of hot milk, a sugarbowl. There were two packets of cigarettes still in their cellophane, French and American, on a white saucer. He took his place at the table. The warmth of the coffee and milk, the still unmelted butter, were evidence that this breakfast had been set down but moments ago, that elsewhere in the house people invisibly moved in his interest. He considered this for a while and decided that it didn't disturb him; or rather, he was less disturbed by the idea than he found it easy to acquiesce to. He accepted that hospitality which is the exacting mercy of strangers. Whatever might become of him now – well, that was what came of staying for breakfast.

In the days that followed he was left much to himself, to come and go as he pleased, in principle at least. The tall, picture-frame windows opening onto the terrace, the golden film-star beach beyond, all without bars, without locks, were a challenge to him, a reminder that were he to leave he had nowhere to go.

He slept for fourteen or sixteen hours a day, in bed or on the beach or on a thick rug in front of the television in the big white room. In the intervals between sleep and sleep he swam in the pool or in the unheated, unventilated sea itself, or took long luxurious baths after which he lay around swathed in towels and watched parts of video films. Also he drank, not in the crazed, gulping manner of old, but steadily through the afternoons. His taste in drinks modified likewise in accordance with his new circumstances: he sipped Benedictine or Irish malt whiskey or bottle on bottle of Piper Heidsieck champagne. His hangovers were less severe.

Carlos was seldom there; it was almost as if he visited his own house only to check how his guest was faring. When they talked, over snack lunches of cheese and grapes out on the terrace, or of an evening when Carlos stopped by to change clothes or snatch a drink before heading back out to that eventful and secret life of his, the discussion was all of needs and practicalities: what Daniel required, which foods, new videos or music. There was no talk nor question of Daniel's leaving, as indeed why should there be, so finely attuned and effortless was his existence there. Daniel fell in with the tacit understanding that he was staying. And after all, he reminded himself, why should his rescuer be motivated by sheer benevolence, why should he not exact a price?

On one such occasion Carlos, looking away, overly casual, enquired if he *needed something*, by which Daniel understood him to mean drugs. Feeling quite all right physically, and recognising a comparatively painless opportunity to assert himself and his own will, he refused, going so far as to frown with displeasure as if the very suggestion were offensive. Nevertheless he knew his reaction for what it was, something quite arbitrary, knew that if Carlos had chosen another moment, or even other words in which to

175

frame his question, he might well have seized on the offer with alacrity and gratitude.

Four days later Luc called up. Daniel wanted him very much to ask for details, at the very least to express surprise, instead of which there on the end of the phone was Luc, cheery, blasé, insultingly uninterested: it was Carlos he wanted to speak to, he explained, there was a message from Saskia, while all the time Daniel was crying out silently, I did all this for you, to be like you. Even so the two boys made an appointment to meet at a seafront bar that afternoon, where Luc chattered on inconsequentially about a planned trip to North Africa and Daniel's adventure was, it seemed, already old news. Thirsty to the last for Luc's approval, Luc's reaction, Daniel took advantage of a lull in the conversation to tell his friend, with desperately forced chagrin: 'You see, Luc. I ended up staying for breakfast.' But Luc, far from being flattered to hear his old aphorism flourished back at him, seemed uncomfortable, and swiftly began speaking of something else; while his eyes avoided Danny's and searched out something invisible on the impassive Mediterranean horizon.

The following week, prodding about amongst some old style magazines under Carlos' coffee table, he found an album of photographs of very young boys, nude or at best scantily clothed in bright bathing trunks, little shorts, loose white vests. As specimens of amateur photography they were really quite accomplished, and Daniel turned the stiff cardboard pages with detached interest and a certain admiration both for the technique, and for the firmness of purpose which alone could have persuaded these models to submit so willingly to the fantasies required of them. Looking closer – for the surface variety was almost sufficient to conceal the pictures' depressing uniformity – Daniel realised that the fantasy depended on, subsisted in this very submission, the extinction of personality in these poses and smiles no boy could have come by naturally. Had Carlos deliberately left out the album for him to find? It was the kind of thing Carlos might well do, though with what motive? – to excite him, remind him of his place, warn him of his future? While significantly none of the photos carried names, there was an unequal representation within Carlos' anonymous harem, and when some favourite was accorded the dubious privilege of three or even four pictures, Daniel experienced a quickening of jealousy even as he recoiled from the whole sordid enterprise. For the first time it occurred to him that if one cannot love what is not lovable, one can all too easily envy the unenviable.

Some of the boys in that album had been little older than Guy was now. Daniel lay on the soft, too-soft hotel bed and wondered about Guy. (And he was never to learn, nor Guy to tell, what little originality there was in the refinements of Carlos' hospitality; how, as with Daniel that summer, so with the ransomed Guy in London; how, during the boy's captivity, Carlos had ensured that certain adult magazines and adult videos be made available and to hand, randomly scattered among the legitimate cassettes, as if there by chance or oversight, for Guy to examine or ignore as he chose, never forced upon him nor even pointed out, but simply provided with patient faith in the inevitable corruptibility of children.)

He wondered if Carlos were really capable of harming his nephew. Partly from a need to reassure himself, partly from a common failing of imagination which induces us to judge others according as they treat ourselves alone, he decided that it was impossible. The Carlos who had raised him from the swimming bathroom floor in Cap d'Agde, who had lavished on him so many kindnesses, shown him such delicacy, worked up such touching compliments and devised such exquisite adventures to give him pleasure, the Carlos who had rescued him from a dozen nightclub brawls, nursed him through a score of tearful or bleeding dawns, who had stood bail against the legion deaths and mutilations he might otherwise have incurred, could not harm a child, much less a child of his, Daniel's, family. But in this he mistook the nature of these kindnesses, measuring them against his own need rather than against the relative ease with which they were Carlos' to dispense, just as he misunderstood the magnanimity whereby Carlos accepted, welcomed even, each one of his errings and crises, since they bound Daniel tighter to him. He misunderstood – or allowed himself to do so, too troubling was it to admit that the very matter sustaining him was the exclusivity of Carlos' fondness for him, its arbitrary and unique character. If Daniel were honest he could find no evidence to suppose that this psychopathic tenderness need extend beyond himself to include any one of those he held dear, for it was a tenderness lifted clear of all values, impelled not by reason but by a personal, even selfish, rationale. Carlos could quite well have harmed Guy without that kindness being in any way diminished, as a man who, sparing one that has caught and charmed his eye, might yet without compunction slaughter the rest of the litter for considerations of space and time.

He made his way down to the street. Well, Guy was far away now, all of them: his mother, his sister, the children, were far away, and he was back in a Paris of old lovers, old creditors. Nor was it merely a question of the distance he had put between them. Already the life he had known in Oxfordshire was receding into blurry unreality, its cosy scenes taking on the glow of a magic lantern tableau; a few more days and he would be able to brush them from his head like the trailing ends of a cobwebbed dream. Not forgetting alone, but the immobilisation of the very processes of memory, had been his purpose when first he fled from England and embarked on the excesses that followed; and in executing this flight he had displayed the same unconsidered instinct of a cat who seeks out the grass that will induce vomiting. But where the cat requires only to expel some alien poison or irritant, what Daniel sought to purge from himself was the very matter of his being.

Tenderness and cruelty: Carlos was quite capable of either, and therein perhaps lay the secret of their attachment. For tenderness and cruelty, each born of an exquisite knowledge of the other's vulnerability, are what a child feels and responds to, the black and white of the colour-blind's vision, while the complex emotions – pride, regard, ambition – are reserved for the adult world. It was the deficit of tenderness in Daniel's life that had left him a retard, emotionally atrophied; that had driven him to prostitution – not in its banal mercantile aspect, but as a prostitute paid in affection, most inflationary of currencies.

It would only be a matter of time before he was one of those faded youths of the Riviera, helplessly adhering to his little routine of breakfast here, an aperitif there, dinner in some indulgent restaurant where the waiters all knew him by name; avoiding sudden movements, absent-minded of conversation, given to repeat or forget himself, but so mild, so docile, so deferential in manner, so much the well-raised, well-dressed, well-spoken young man who, should his parents ever venture so far, would immediately surrender them a terrace table or offer them a seat on a tram – so much, in short, the kind of boy they would have liked to have. And in this they would have won. Winners and losers, parents and children: we are not after all so very far removed from those dynastic conflicts of mythological Greece, when the parents conspired against the children, and the children avenged themselves on the parents; and our contests today are not the less absolute in that the prize is no longer earthly sway or heavenly dominion, but sanity.

His taxi dropped him at Saint Michel, and he stood there for a brief moment on the damp pavement in front of the café. People jostled him as they passed, and their utter indifference to him was a source of comfort. Comforting, too, the scene that presented itself behind those windows. How warm the café looked, how opulent, how hospitable its hundred lamps burning over the intimate groups cosy around their glasses and carafes! How at peace its customers appeared, weaving conversation, conducting business or affairs, suffused with this glow of warmth and refuge. He knew they were not all nice people such as this tableau made them out to be, knew that some of them were malignant, some desperate, others criminal. But in this

179

moment they formed an oddly harmonious and appealing picture, and he no longer felt incongruous standing there, a little middle-class English boy from a good university. His mind was absolutely clear, his hands no longer trembled. He pushed open the glass door and scanned the faces that turned towards him for one he recognised. But the faces were all familiar, and all looked as if they knew him.

☐ Tommy Was Here	Simon Corrigan	£5.99
☐ A Summer Tide	Tony Peake	£5.99
☐ The Water People	Joe Simpson	£5.99
☐ My House is on Fire	Ariel Dorfman	£5.99
☐ The Seduction of Morality	Tom Murphy	£5.99
☐ The Moon Rising	Steve Kelly	£5.99

Abacus now offers an exciting range of quality titles by both established and new authors which can be ordered from the following address:

Little, Brown & Company (UK),
P.O. Box 11,
Falmouth,
Cornwall TR10 9EN.

Alternatively you may fax your order to the above address.
Fax No. 01326 317444.

Payments can be made as follows: cheque, postal order (payable to Little, Brown and Company) or by credit cards, Visa/Access. Do not send cash or currency. UK customers and B.F.P.O. please allow £1.00 for postage and packing for the first book, plus 50p for the second book, plus 30p for each additional book up to a maximum charge of £3.00 (7 books plus). Overseas customers including Ireland, please allow £2.00 for the first book plus £1.00 for the second book, plus 50p for each additional book.

NAME (Block Letters)_____

ADDRESS _____

_____

_____

☐ I enclose my remittance for £_____
☐ I wish to pay by Access/Visa Card

Number ☐☐☐☐☐☐☐☐☐☐☐☐☐☐☐☐

Card Expiry Date _____